The
LIGHTKEEPER'S
DAUGHTER

IAIN LAWRENCE

The
LIGHTKEEPER'S DAUGHTER

Delacorte Press

Published by
Delacorte Press
an imprint of
Random House Children's Books
a division of Random House, Inc.
1540 Broadway
New York, New York 10036

Visit us on the Web! www.randomhouse.com/teens
Educators and librarians, for a variety of teaching tools, visit us at
www.randomhouse.com/teachers

Library of Congress Cataloging-in-Publication Data

Lawrence, Iain.
    The Lightkeeper's daughter / Iain Lawrence.
        p.   cm.
Summary: When, after a four-year absence, seventeen-year-old Squid returns
to her childhood home on a remote lighthouse island off British Columbia
with her young daughter in tow, she and her parents try to come to terms
with each other and the painful events of the past, especially the death of
her older brother.
    ISBN 0-385-72925-1 (trade)—ISBN 0-385-90062-7 (lib. bdg.)
    [1. Family problems—Fiction. 2. Brothers and sisters—Fiction.
3. Lighthouse keepers—Fiction. 4. Islands—Fiction.
5. British Columbia—Fiction.] I. Title.
    PZ7.L43545 Li 2002
    [Fic]—dc21
                                                    2002000578
The text of this book is set in 12-point Goudy.
Book design by Melissa J Knight

Printed in the United States of America
September 2002
10 9 8 7 6 5 4 3 2 1
BVG

For Sheila,
who drew the map that guided me to Lucy Island
and encouraged me from the beginning

chapter one

*I*N THE BOW OF THE SHIP, HIGH ABOVE THE sea, stands a girl of seventeen. She looks like a figurehead carved from wood, her arms never moving, her hair chiseled in place and painted with gold.

The ship carries her north at the speed of the wind, as though forever in a calm. The flags at the mast are twists of limp cloth, the smoke a gray column rising straight from the funnel. It's the sea, not the ship, that appears to be moving. It bursts on the bow and roars down the sides in tumbling foam. It carries rafts of torn kelp and logs that tilt through the waves. Seagulls and auklets skitter away, but the girl stares only ahead.

At her side is her daughter, dressed all in red. Too small to see over the rail, she crouches instead on the deck, peering through the oval of the hawsehole. Her tiny hands are cupped on the metal, and she stares out between them, the way a cat watches from a windowsill. Wedged between her knees is a red plastic purse, its flap buttoned across a Barbie doll too long to fit inside. A frizzy head juts out from one end, a pair of pink feet from the other.

The sea marches past, bashing at the bow, flinging droplets of spray that skitter like beetles on the water. It surges below the girl standing there, now reaching toward her, now falling away as the ship, meeting a wave, rises to the crest. And far ahead a tiny bright cap appears on the skyline. A single white eye blinks at her over all the miles of water.

In a moment it's gone, lost in the waves as the ship drops from the crest, as the foam at the bow billows toward her. But the girl watches and waits, and again it appears, the little red cap, the blink of the light. It's what she's been watching for ever since the *Darby* turned at the Kinahan Islands an hour ago. And at last she moves. She raises a hand and covers her mouth.

The island seems to rise from the sea like a surfacing whale. Trees and rocks appear, veiled in a silver of spindrift and mist. A tower forms below the red cap, at first so tiny and white that it makes the girl think of a gravestone. Then buildings emerge, red roofs and white walls. Squares of green lawn. Dark swaths of salal.

Each little piece fills the girl with a particular feeling, with a picture in her mind, or a smell or a sound. She was born on that island; she's the lightkeeper's daughter. Her name is Elizabeth McCrae, but all her life she's been known as Squid.

"Tatiana, look," she says. "That's Lizzie Island there."

The child doesn't answer. She seldom speaks. Her little shoulders are bent, her head thrust forward. She's always been small for her age, but now she looks tiny and fragile, closer to two than to three. Squid settles beside her, on the gray steel of the deck. She holds on to Tatiana as though the child might slide through the hole and into the sea.

Tatiana looks up, her eyes jiggling, all her teeth showing in her peculiar grin.

"You doing okay?" asks Squid.

Tatiana nods.

"We're almost there. You'll meet your grandma and your grandpa. They've got a boat with a glass bottom, and a little tractor that can pull you in a wagon."

Squid wants to tell her everything: about Glory, the little winged horse; about Gomorrah and the wailing wall; about Alastair's flute and the singing of whales. But Tatiana isn't listening. The child has already turned back to the hawsehole, watching the water rush past the boat.

<hr>

On the island, the wind feels brisk. It drives the waves against the shore and shreds them into spray. It gusts up the rocks and over the sodden lawn, where Murray McCrae, the lightkeeper, stands in his khaki shorts.

"*Darby*'s coming," he says, making it sound as though he doesn't care, as though he hasn't been watching for the ship since dawn first came to Lizzie Island. In his hands he holds the things the sea has cast ashore: strands of kelp and bits of bark and sticks like old men's fingers, warted with barnacle shells.

Six feet behind him, Hannah looks up and turns toward the sun. It's well to the south so late in September, and it glares off the waves, off the rocks wet with spray. She squints, then puts her hands to her face and peers through the tunnel made by her fingers, the shape of a heart on the sea.

The *Darby* is far in the distance. A plume of brown smoke, a speck of red for the hull. Her daughter's out there, an hour away.

Murray carries his sticks to the edge of the grass and heaves them back where they came from, over the cliff and down to the sea. He claps his hands together, then hitches up his shorts. "Better get hopping," he says. "I've got things to do. Sand to carry."

In a moment he's off on his little tractor, bulging above it like a circus bear. A rickety cart, rusted and squeaking, bounces behind him as he rattles down the boardwalk and into the forest.

Hannah goes the other way, over the trestle and up through the tower, out at the top to the platform that circles it. For nearly a week, a lone humpback whale has been feeding on the shallows off the island, and she looks for it now as she might watch from a porch for a friend passing by. The wind buffets at the long, dark dress of the lightkeeper's wife, at the crimson scarf tied round her hair.

Once this was her favorite place, above the houses and the patch of emerald lawn. Ringed in by the railing, she was never frightened by the height, though she stood so high above the sea that the birds flew below her and the surf flickered white on the distant reefs of Devil Rock. Autumn, once, was her favorite time, a summer's end when the whales and the birds stopped to rest on their southward migrations. But now the island is a prison, and the sea a wall around it. Autumn is the start of winter and the coming of the Undertaker. Even the wind makes her frightened.

She believes now that it has a voice. She has heard it often in the last three years—as a breath in the summer's tall grass, as a whisper through the forest of moss-bearded trees. It has shouted her name in the storms that come from the south, when the gulls are flung through the sky like scraps of paper. She hasn't told Murray any of this, but the voice on the wind is their son's.

Yesterday he was there. When the storm was at its peak and the house rattled and shook, when the Canadian flag tore itself into streamers of red and white, she looked out and saw him in the flash of the light. He was gone in the darkness that followed: there and then gone. Poor Alastair—four years drowned—blown up from the sea in the storm.

Hannah shudders, remembering that, her vision of him. She moves back from the rail and leans on the glass. Though eighty feet above the sea, it's stained with salt, remnants of last night's storm. Hannah rubs at the white splotches with her hand, and then with the scarf, tearing it off to let her hair blow in tangles. Every five seconds, the light flashes in the cupola.

It's a pathetic thing now, that light, a plastic dome on a little stick of a pole. The old lantern is long gone, the one that floated in its mercury bath, going round and around with a brilliance brighter than sunlight.

"Don't look straight at it," Murray told her the first time he took her up to the tower. "It could burn out your eyes," he said. And for a week after that she went back and forth over the lawns with her eyes squinted, until Murray—laughing—told her how the beam passed far above. But it cast her shadow on the grass, a gray shape that leapt beside her as she walked. It flashed in through the windows and followed her down through the forest. It was like an enormous eye up there, watching her always. And she was glad when the new one came, though Murray hated it right from the start.

"Look at the bulbs," he said. "The wee little bulbs." He lifted off the plastic dome and she saw them underneath, half a dozen bulbs in a gizmo of metal and plastic. They were the size of Christmas tree lights.

"It's the start of the end," said Murray. "They'll get rid of the keepers next, just you wait and see." Then he reached out and loosened the bulb. A moment later the holder turned by itself. The old bulb swung down and a new one rose in its place with a whir and a click. She heard the little crackle as the filament glowed white-hot.

"Give it a year," said Murray. "And we'll get our walking papers then."

Well, many years have passed and the walking papers still haven't arrived. Murray dreads their coming, but Hannah looks forward to it.

She rubs at the salt, and the glass quivers under her hand when the humpback breathes. The sound comes to her like a bang of metal, and she turns her head in time to see a plume of spray shimmer in the sun, a cloud as thin as kettle steam. A dozen gulls tumble toward it, where the water is dark and swirling. Hannah searches among the rocks, in the channel where the water is gold and silver from the sand. She searches to the south, but she doesn't find the whale.

Only the *Darby* is out there, bringing her daughter in a traveling smoke, like old Yahweh looming up from the desert. Puffs of spray rise from the bow, white flowers blooming, as though the ship is steaming through a field of dandelions. For a moment, Hannah wishes for the binoculars. They hang from a peg beside the door, next to a little brown envelope that Murray has glued there to hold his lens-cleaning papers. But the wish soon passes. They are big German binoculars that once peered from a U-boat, or so Murray told her. She's afraid of them in a way, frightened that she might see the things they have seen if she holds them just so in her hands. And no, she decides, it would be wrong to watch for her daughter through lenses that have witnessed the drowning of men.

Below her, across the bridge and over the lawn, Murray's tractor comes puttering back along the path. The engine coughs and stops. It's his third day of hauling sand, two buckets at a time.

On the first day she asked him, "Why can't the child just play at the beach?"

"They like their sand in boxes," he said. "Cats and babies, you know." He shrugged. "Och, they're pretty much the same."

He's never had a cat; he's never met Tatiana.

"And see?" he said. "I've made some toys for the lassie."

They're lovely things, built of chunky wood that's red and yellow. There's a boat just like the *Darby*, with a crane to lift tiny chests from the deck. There's a sailboat and a freighter, and a flat-topped ferry with three funny-looking cars that drive aboard on sliding ramps.

"What sort of cars are those?" she asked.

"Och, I don't know," he said. "I was thinking of DeSotos."

Now Hannah smiles to herself. Murray hasn't seen a car in nearly twenty-five years.

She watches, from her height, as he lifts the buckets one at a time from the wagon and empties them into the sandbox. He stoops to one knee and smooths out the pile, sifting through it for clamshells and stones and bits of glass, which he drops in a bucket to put back on the beach. His hand moves, his fingers open, and the sound of the things hitting the bucket reaches her long after, when he's already sifting again. Then he glances up, past the little shed he's built around the sandbox, and he stands with the buckets in his hands.

He's keeping a watch on the *Darby*, Hannah can see, as he bustles around, pretending not to care. He carries his buckets to the tractor, and glances to the south. He puts them into the wagon and glances again. Then off he goes to the big house, to watch from the windows, she thinks. And, sure enough, he doesn't appear again until the ship is turning toward the channel.

The smoke from the funnel now streams to the side, and the white strip of foam at the bow thins to a sliver as the *Darby* slows for the run toward shore. Hannah can see people on the deck, but she can't make out her daughter. She waves, both arms going wildly from side to side, the long scarf flapping from her fingers.

The whistle shrieks. Two shrill blasts.

She follows the ship around the tower, smiling and crying. Close up it's enormous, ugly now, streaked with trickles of rust. The smoke blows around her, warm and oily.

She tugs at the door at the top of the tower. The wind pushes against it, then slams it behind her as she slips through the gap. She clatters down the stairs and out the bottom, across the trestle from crag to island, down the path that Murray built to keep footprints off the lawn.

He's already busy with the winch when she comes up beside him. The derrick is swung out, the hook dangling above the sea. He's peering down from his platform, watching the *Darby* pick up the mooring buoy. Men in orange life jackets move across the deck, launching the workboat, stacking boxes by the rail.

And there's Squid! She looks so tall, so beautiful, standing at the gap in the rail, leaning on the little fence of painted chain. It's almost a shock to Hannah to see her daughter as a woman. She'd been expecting the same girl she'd last seen in a little house in Prince Rupert. But Tatiana! Hannah frowns: *Oh, what is Squid thinking?* she wonders. In her solid red clothes, the child looks like one of the figures on Murray's whirligigs.

"Och, look at the pair of them," says Murray. "How old is Tatiana now?"

"Don't worry," says Hannah. "She's not too old to play in the sand."

Murray seems nervous. He scratches his arm, then raises a knee and scratches his leg. His skin is burned to a rosy pink below the hem of his shorts. Every inch of him is mottled with freckles and covered in a thin bright sheen of coppery hairs.

"I should have put on trousers," he says.

"You're fine," Hannah tells him.

Squid has never come to the island this way. She has never seen it from the height of the *Darby's* deck. Now it seems smaller than she remembers, the trees crowding more closely around the houses and the lawns. The tower has shrunk. The islets and reefs that had stretched on forever now huddle close by.

"Squid?" A Coast Guard crewman touches her arm. He stands almost astride Tatiana, as though the child isn't there. "You'll have to move down the deck," he says. "We're tying to the buoy, okay?"

He's old, she thinks. Maybe forty. There is white in his hair, like chalk scribbled on a blackboard. If she knew him before, she doesn't remember. "Okay," she says. "Sure." But she stays in the bow as the *Darby* passes the tower, until she sees her mother up there, waving like a madwoman, with a red scarf as long as the wind sock. Then she hears a laugh from one of the men and, embarrassed, looks down at her daughter. "Come on, Tat. Let's go."

Tatiana stands up, fiddling with her purse, straightening the Barbie doll inside. Her little fingers work clumsily; her face is set in a serious frown.

Squid stands above her, waiting until the child looks up. "Ready?" she asks, and Tatiana nods. Squid leads her by the hand, over the anchor chain and round the windlass, down to the gap in the rail that's fenced with sagging chains.

The men busy themselves with the boat and the lighthouse supplies. A circle of gulls wheels overhead, but Squid watches only the island, seeing the rocks go by, and then the concrete steps that climb from the sea. Stained black at the bottom, thick with weeds and dangling kelp, they rise to a sun-baked whiteness, turning once to reach the platform at the top, where her father is pushing out the derrick. In his wide-legged shorts and flame of red hair he looks oddly out of place, and just seeing him makes Squid want to laugh and cry at the same time, to run toward him and run away.

She holds on to Tatiana. "You stay with me," she says.

Tatiana is staring at the water. She's reaching down between the chains, her arm stretching out, her fingers spread open. Squid tightens her grip and peers over the side. A strand of kelp, broken loose, is drifting past the ship. "That's only seaweed," she says.

"Coming," whispers Tatiana.

"Who?"

"Hear him," she says.

"Who?" asks Squid again. Then Tatiana's whole weight is suddenly in her hand. The child gropes toward the water, struggling to get closer, to climb between the two chains. Her little red shirt stretches in Squid's fist.

"Tat!"

And up from the sea comes the whale. It's enormous

and dark, wrapped in a cascade of white. Water pours from its mouth, from plates of baleen, down ribbons of flesh that are mottled and brown. And still the whale rises, arching above them, an eye and a throat and a long curving fin that is studded with barnacles all down its length.

Its breath comes in a cloud, in a rain smelling of old rotting fish. Its eye swivels round, and the whale seems to hang there, higher by half than the height of the deck. Then, with impossible slowness, it rolls onto its back and crashes into the sea.

"Holy smokes," says Squid, in a whisper.

For a long time, nobody moves. The Coast Guard crew stand at their winches, at their ropes and controls. The sea ripples and swirls, and the screaming gulls swoop. And Tatiana, with her eyes closed, trembles all over.

⌒

Hannah sees the humpback coming through the shallows, a huge black shadow on the silver and the gold. She sees Tatiana fling herself against the chain, and then the sea erupts and the whale breaches, blotting out the girl. Its flippers are long and slender, vast as wings. They curl and twist as the whale rolls sideways and plunges down.

A wave rolls out and breaks against the cliff. It surges on the little sandy beach, climbs two—then three—of the concrete steps. The humpback spouts farther down the channel, and again at the shallow bar toward the sea. Then it is gone, and the gulls go with it, dipping down each time it rises, feeding in its wake. And everything is silent; everyone is still as stone.

Murray is gazing down with tears in his eyes. Hannah sees him crying and looks away; she can imagine what he's thinking. There hasn't been a whale in the shallow waters of the channel since Alastair died.

"Miraculous," he says.

That one word carries her back twenty years, to her first autumn on the island. She remembers how she and Murray sat on the platform at the tower's top, watching the humpbacks swimming. They swam in a sea of blood at the setting of the sun, surfacing together, breathing together, their spouts joining in a single cloud.

"Humpbacks sing," said Murray. "Did you know that?"

She shook her head.

"Each year one of them starts a song. Then others pick it up; they lengthen it and change it." He spoke softly—he always did—looking out to sea and not at her. "By the middle of summer they all know the song. They sing in a chorus over hundreds of miles."

She leaned her head against his shoulder. She could feel him breathing, and she tried to do what the whales were doing, and time her breath to his.

"No one knew," said Murray. "Until the war. Then someone put a microphone in the water, hoping to hear submarines. They heard this singing instead. And they didn't know what the hell it was."

She pressed herself against him. She was shivering, but he didn't notice.

"I don't understand it," he said.

"The song?" she asked.

He shook his head. "Och, we'll never understand that. I mean how men could kill them."

"No," she said.

He sighed. "They're wonderful things, whales are. They're miraculous."

chapter two

THE SUPPLIES ARE UNLOADED AND FERRIED to shore. Boxes of groceries, barrels of fuel, library books and cans of white paint, they're all winched up the bluff and onto the landing. Murray makes pyramids from the boxes, and perfect columns from the paint cans.

He shouts down from his platform, "Is that the lot of it then?" And a voice calls back, "Just the girls left, Mr. McCrae."

He insists that the Coast Guard calls him that. Even Hannah called him that the first time, when he ran before her—absolutely naked—and came back with his shirt buttoned in all the wrong holes. "I'm Hannah," she said, and held out her hand. "I'm Mr. McCrae," he told her. She thought it was a bit of old world dignity, but now she knows he's claiming title to his island. It pleases him to see a man in uniform subservient. If he'd thought of it, she imagines, he would have told them all, "My name is Lord McCrae."

"We'd better get down there, Murray," she says.

"Yes," he tells her. "I'll be along. I just have to put the winch away."

This morning his fussiness annoys her. She would like to leave him there, but can't. The boat will bring Squid to the concrete stairs, and she won't go down alone. She hates those stairs that fall right down the cliff and into the water, vanishing in a murk of green and blue. Squid, as a child, would sit there with her feet in the swell, chattering on and on about how much she would like to walk right to the bottom, to hold her breath and go down, to stroll among the starfish and the crabs. But Hannah stays clear of the stairs, and won't go near the place after dark. It scares her to think what might come walking up them from the sea: a drowned boy, bloated and white, squelching in the algae.

"Murray," she says.

"Coming." He swings the derrick into place. He lowers the hook, snaps it to its loop of rope, then pulls it tight. He sets the controls exactly in the middle, then tests each one three times. "Right," he says. "Right. Let's go." And he stoops to turn a cardboard box an inch to the left, in line with another below it.

There's no railing on the steps. Hannah walks down the middle, right behind Murray, and they stop at the landing and wait side by side. For some reason it takes three men to bring Squid to shore. They stand as straight as admirals, each one in a pale blue shirt, in dark and ironed trousers. The bowman grabs for a hold with a metal-tipped boat hook, and it clangs and rasps over the concrete. The boat washes up against the steps, tilts, and washes back.

"Careful," shouts Hannah. The steps are slick at the bottom, the concrete chipped at the corners by the battering of logs. She fears that Squid will slide right off them, dragging Tatiana behind her. She clings to Murray—to solid, fearless Murray.

Squid is beautiful—all rosy and tanned. The men in the boat hover around her as she lifts Tatiana across to the steps. They lean with her, reaching out as the water licks at her shoes, and finally their hands fall away as she comes hurrying up to the landing. She lifts her head and looks up, and in her eyes Hannah sees disappointment. It flashes there for only an instant before it's hidden by a smile. But Hannah sees it, and she isn't surprised.

Murray is sixty-two now, getting fat where he never was before. His legs are chubby and pink. The sun and the wind have worn him smooth, but they have chiseled away at Hannah, carving deep lines in her face. She and Murray must look older than they should.

It's an awkward moment when they all stand together, though Hannah fears that it's hardest on Murray. Squid is so changed, so much a woman, that she isn't the least like his daughter. She steps toward him only to balk back. And then nobody moves, until *everyone* moves, and they tangle like trees in a gale before they all step away, breathing heavily.

Squid reaches behind her and drags out Tatiana. She thrusts the child forward. "Say hello," she says, "to your grandma and your grandpa."

Murray squats down, his pink legs bulging. "Hello, Tatiana," he says.

The child turns crimson, and thrusts her fingers into her mouth.

"We saw the whale," says Murray. "Did he give you a fright, the big beastie?"

Tatiana sits down. She swings her red purse into her lap, and unfastens the top.

"What's that you've got there?" asks Murray.

Squid says, like a song, "That's her Barbie doll there."

Murray reaches for it, but Tatiana pulls it away. "Well," he says. "That's sure a nice Barney doll." And he stands, embarrassed and bewildered.

Below them, the boat backs off from the steps. The men stare up. They call out to Squid; only to her. "Good luck," says one. "See you in a month," says another. And Hannah catches the look Squid gives them, a smile that's almost a grimace.

"A month?" says Murray.

"Yes, I'll stay the month," says Squid.

"And no more than that?"

"Let's not talk about that now." She stoops, takes Tatiana's hand, and starts up the steps.

"They're slippery," says Hannah. "And there's no railing to hold." Her heart is in her mouth; if the child were to slip she'd crack open her skull. "Go slowly, for heaven's sake."

Squid looks back, laughing in a way that Hannah finds annoying. For such a beautiful girl, Squid has an ugly laugh.

Murray goes slowly, boosting himself up each concrete step by pressing his hands on his thighs. Once he would have sprinted, carrying Squid in one arm and Alastair in the other, twirling at the top, balancing right at the edge.

The children would have squealed with delight as he all but dangled them over the brink. Hannah, coming behind him, is glad those days are over.

But Squid is impatient. "I'm going to run ahead," she says. "I want to show Tat my old room."

Then she's gone, pulling Tatiana by the hand. She skips up the steps and vanishes on the level ground.

Murray bends forward and hurries a bit. Hannah sees the look in his eyes and knows what he's thinking. He's worried about his grass seed; the ground is nearly bare at the top of the steps. No matter what he tells them, everyone walks on the lawn. So he boosts himself up a step, up another, before he slows again.

"Och," he says. "I can't keep up."

Hannah wants to march up the steps and tell Squid to go back. They might all have walked together, she thinks. But Murray's looking pained, and she doesn't want to leave him. She'd like to comfort him, but isn't sure what to say. She could tell him that reunions are hard, that everything will be just fine as soon as Squid settles in.

But she isn't sure that it's true.

⌒

On posts and pillars, nailed to the trunks of trees, Murray's whirligigs flutter and jerk in gusts of wind as Squid hurries by. A wooden lady throws her weight against a pump and then rests on the handle; two little men rock lazily with a bucksaw between them; a lion tamer holds his whip high over two golden lions faded to yellow.

There was a time when Squid lay for hours watching these things. Horses ran in an endless race. Sailboats tacked for miles and miles on a squeaky, rusted pivot. Alastair was beside her when they imagined themselves at the controls of the little airplane, cranking the propeller and flapping the wings, flying off to places they had never seen.

She almost drags Tatiana behind her, past the light-keeper's house and on down a pathway of gravel and shells, past the sundial, past the flat wooden horse gallop-ing into the wind.

There are only two houses on Lizzie Island. The second is smaller, so glaringly white that the gleam of the flower box shimmers on the wall like northern lights. It was built for a junior keeper, but there never was one who lasted more than a week on the island. In Squid's early childhood they came like a parade—lonely young men who could never match Murray's high standards. They would come on one boat and be off on the next, often without unpacking their bags. Then the house sat empty, until Alastair first—and Squid a year later—celebrated turning twelve by moving down the path to the house they called Gomorrah.

"I love that name," said Alastair. He said it loudly, like a battle cry. "Gomorrah!" he shouted again. "It's where the patriarchs settled when they needed more room. It was a place of their own by themselves."

He was a genius, poor Alastair. He was always reading, forever with a book in his hand. He could talk about kings and queens as though he'd known them, about history as if he'd seen it. And everything he read he remembered.

"You've got so much in your head," Squid told him once, "that it keeps leaking out of your mouth."

The sign is still there, nailed over the door, that terrible name written in black on a bit of pale wood. He painted it the day he moved in, his head bent so close to the wood that his hand kept bumping his nose.

"I'm myopic," he told her. "Probably I'll be blind before I'm thirty."

He had only just got his glasses, after years of squinting at everything. Murray had always said he didn't need them. "McCraes have never worn spectacles." That was what Murray said. "The sea, the sun, the air: It's better than any doctor."

Squid sighs and opens the door. The knob works so well that she knows at once that her father keeps it oiled. She steps into a big front room that hasn't changed in a single way. Her yellow raincoat is hanging on its hook, Alastair's beside it. Their boots stand underneath. Their chairs are pulled up to a table covered with books in neat stacks, with the shells that Squid had been lacing together into a necklace meant for her mother.

"That was Alastair's chair," says Squid. "The one under the lamp." She lets go of Tatiana's hand, and closes the door behind her. "He got the best chair, and the best room, because he was here first."

The year they spent apart was the worst of any for Squid. Although they were together almost as much as before, from morning to dark, she felt lonely and—separate. Every night, she marked off another day on the calendar, and went to bed crying.

"The pair of you are like Siamese twins," Murray told her. "Joined together in every way but time." He sat on her bed, facing the wall, and told her, "You've no idea how short a year is. Why, it's just a drop in a bucket."

But it seemed forever. And then, on her birthday, Alastair came to carry her things. They made four trips, back and forth like ants, downstairs and up, one with a table and one with a chair, then each with a box, each with another, each with a bundle of clothes. Alastair made tea and, clinking his cup against hers, said, "Welcome to Gomorrah." And when they finished, he put his nose almost in the cup to look at the patterns that the leaves had left.

He said, "Yours looks like a dancer. It's happy and laughing. Well, that fits," he said. "And see, mine is a kayak."

"Oh, you're just seeing what you want to see," said Squid.

"I guess so," he said, and laughed. "But look. My kayak's upside down."

⌒

He was fourteen when he died, a year and a day older than Squid. The sound of his flute came through the trees that November night, and she went from her bed to her window, as though she might see the notes that he played flitting through the darkness. She could hear the surf— there was a swell heaving against the island, though not a breath of wind to drive it—and she thought of him out there in his kayak, alone in the night as he so often was.

She imagined his paddles flashing green with phosphorescence, and she closed her eyes and listened.

It was a strange music of whistles and shrieks—not songs at all; he never played songs. On a night that was eerily calm, the sound of his flute was a howling of wind.

It was whale music. He played with the whales, or *for* the whales; Squid even then wasn't sure. Yet Alastair thought he *talked* with the whales, that he understood the language in their songs. And he played, then listened, and wrote down in a battered, water-stained book the things he heard in this singing of whales.

That night he played without stopping. That night the humpbacks vanished, fattened for the long swim to Hawaii. Alastair's strange, warbling song was cheerful and fast, then dismally sad. And Squid, her fingers on the window glass, thought that at last she understood. He was telling his own story in the way of the whales, and she heard him speak of laughter and sadness and dreams.

In the morning they found his kayak drifting in the channel north of the lighthouse. It was upside down, turning in the tide, coming in from the sea through the tangle of rocks. It spun past an island, past a reef, in through the gap to the little lagoon, where the sun turned the water to diamonds.

⌐⌐

The house now seems empty and cold. But for Squid, the voices are as much a part of it as the worn spots on the arms of the chairs, as the scraped-away paint on the floor by the steps. Everywhere she looks, she hears them. She sees herself sprawled on the seat of the big dormer window, Alastair standing beside her.

"I'm starting to see how it works," he said. He was talking about whales. "They don't use words so much. It's ideas. Like pictures in sound. Sometimes they talk and I see what they're saying. I *see* it, Squid." He put his hands over his sad, weak eyes. "I see water with the sunshine in it, bits of plankton floating. I see whales all around me, as though I'm one of them. Traveling. Squid, I've seen salmon all shiny and bright. I've seen icebergs. And, listen: I saw *me*."

"You've lost it," she said.

"It's true." He took down his hands, and she saw how his eyes were turning cloudy and white. "They were passing below me, singing away, and I saw myself—the kayak—this shimmering thing against the light on the surface. I was moving the paddle, and I saw that too."

"Sure. Whatever." Squid stared out the window, north across the little islets, into a gray of clouds. She heard the curious sound of Alastair being frustrated. He breathed through his nose, with a whine and a rasp.

He said, "You know the noise a fax machine makes?"

"We don't have one," said Squid.

"But you've *heard* them. On the radio. Whistles and beeps; a pattern of sound that a computer turns into pictures. If you could under*stand* it, you wouldn't *need* the computer; you could see it yourself."

She said, "So get a computer."

"I'm *trying to!*" he said. His voice was full of anguish. "I've been telling him that. I need computers and spectrographs and sound editors. If I had that, I could do it. We could *talk* to the whales."

⌒

Tatiana is staring at her. She's biting her lip, holding her doll in front of her chest.

"Oh, Tat," says Squid. The puzzlement on the child's face makes her laugh. "It's all right, baby. I'm just thinking. I'm just remembering." It seems to her now that she must have been *talking* as well; she has found herself standing in the arc of the window, in the place Alastair had stood before, in that last year of his life.

"Come on," she says. "Let's look upstairs."

Tatiana follows, starting off with a jerk and staying at a distance, as though tied to her mother by a bit of string. She bumps up the stairs, two feet on each step, clinging to the rail.

At the top is a landing, a door on each side. Alastair, choosing first, took the room to the west, with a small window looking over the forest. The other room is larger, and the windows bigger, facing east toward the tower. Squid thought she had got the better room, until darkness came on her first day in Gomorrah, and the glare came in through the window. It lit the room in a pulse of light, and again five seconds later. It flashed through the curtains so brightly that she didn't sleep at all for three nights. Then the fog came in, and she heard her father go out from the house next door to start up the horn. And the blast from it shook the glass in the panes; it shook in her teeth and her jaw. But the fog muted the light, and Squid fell asleep in a moment. She was used to the sound of the horn.

"Here is where I lived," says Squid, opening the next door.

This room, too, is just the same. The bureau drawers poke out at different lengths, bubbling bits of clothing. There's a sweater on the floor and a parka on a chair, and everywhere there's muddle. Only the bed is different, the blankets and sheets torn from the mattress, the pillows scrunched against the headboard.

Suddenly, in the doorway, Squid sees herself fleeing from here, running in her nightgown, screaming down the stairs. She pulls the door shut and pulls it again; it rattles and bangs on its hinges.

Murray catches his breath at the top of the steps. He gazes down at his fresh-seeded grass, at the trails of footprints across a patch of loam. Then he sighs, and sorts out two mismatched suitcases from the neat stacks that he's made at the winch.

"Leave them," says Hannah. "Squid will get them. Squid and me."

"Best do it now," he says. He rubs his hands, then tries to take both the bags at once. He grunts at the weight of them. "Good lord. If I start off now, I might just get them up to the house and back before the boat comes to fetch her again."

Hannah smiles. He won't leave them here; she knows that. She takes one herself, and it saddens her a bit to see that Murray doesn't protest. He goes off at a terrible slant, balancing the weight of his bag with his arm thrust absurdly from his side, his shorts sagging down. She carries the other in front of her, both hands on the straps, taking awkward little steps as the suitcase thumps at her knees. And still he leads her along the path, though a shortcut on the grass would halve the distance to the small house.

They pass the whirligigs without looking, the big house without stopping. In Hannah's mind they're a pair of mules, plodding along without thinking. Her eyes are cast down at the path, watching Murray's heels. Only once does she glance up, to judge the distance left to go.

The small house was empty when she came to the island. It stayed that way for thirteen years, except for the few days at a time when the junior keepers came, nervous as suitors. One of them left in tears. Murray called them dogs. "Lazy, incompetent dogs." All twelve of them were just the same. And then Alastair moved into the house, Squid a year later.

Now it's empty again, a monument to the ruined lives of Lizzie Island. When she follows Murray up the wooden stairs, across the porch to the doorway, it's the first time she's been so close to the house since that nightmarish autumn and the death of her child.

Even now she won't go more than a step through the door. She doesn't close it behind her; she'll never do that. She puts down her suitcase and stays right there, in the sun and the sound of the birds.

It's not the same for Murray. But she knows that Murray visits here. If he comes into the big house through the kitchen door, and goes straight to the sink to splash his face with water, she knows he's been to see Alastair's room.

The floorboards creak upstairs. Murray's head turns to

follow the sound. And down through the ceiling comes Squid's voice, high with excitement.

"He kept a lamp here on the sill," she says. "A storm lantern. Poor Alastair." She laughs. "He hoped that one night the main light would burn out in the tower, and his lantern would save a whole ship from wrecking on the rocks." Her voice fades away. "I don't know what happened to that lantern."

Hannah knows. The old brass lamp sits ready at the window of her own bedroom. Murray keeps the wick trimmed and the glass polished, the bowl full of good, fresh oil. Many times she's wondered why. "It's tradition" was all that Murray ever told her.

Now he blushes.

"And look, Tat. Oh, look!" says Squid. "Here's his flute. He was so good with his flute. Everything he did he was good at."

"That's it," says Murray. He heads for the stairs. "I don't want them fiddling with that."

Squid is still talking. "He could play such amazing things. He played for the whales."

Murray holds on to the newel post. Leaning forward, he bellows up the stairs. "Squid!"

"We'll look later." A door closes and Squid comes bounding down the steps. Tatiana, behind her, totters along with the doll in her fist.

Murray says, "Elizabeth."

Even Hannah is surprised. Squid looks at her father the same way she always did when he used her real name. But now she's close to his own height on level ground, and fairly towers over him from two steps up. She flicks her hair from her shoulder.

He says, "I know you think you've a right to do this, but I'll ask you to respect his things. I don't want anything moved."

She squints and frowns. "Why?" she asks.

"Because I'm asking you." Murray scratches his hair. "For the love of mercy, I don't think it's so much to ask."

"But why?"

Hannah's annoyed by the little upturning lilt in the voice, by the way Squid blinks and tilts her head like a bird.

"Why, Dad?" Squid asks again.

Murray doesn't blink. "Because," he says, "that's the one thing we have left of him. You can understand that, can't you?"

"Well, gee, that's funny," says Squid. "He never let you in there when he was alive. Did he?" Then she pushes past her father, squeezing by with her breasts crushed against his arm, and flounces past Hannah to the porch.

Murray turns to watch her, his face as red as a warning light.

"You see?" Squid looks at Hannah as she passes. "We'd better stick together, Mom. It's the men against the girls."

~

Hannah hasn't forgotten. It's the way it always was. "Men against the girls," Murray would say, and they faced one another across a badminton net, a cribbage board, a line drawn in the sand for tug-of-war. Men against the girls, and they all laughed and shouted as the men, inevitably, beat the girls hollow again.

But Squid never complained. Hannah wouldn't have understood if she had. They were a happy family then. Murray and Alastair were as much friends as they were father and son. Squid and Hannah were the same.

The men against the girls was just the way it was, and Hannah never knew it bothered anyone until the day Squid left the island. There were only three of them on Lizzie then. They stood on the boardwalk as the helicopter settled on the pad, sagging on its wheels like a tired bee. The wind lashed at them in a flurry of twigs and sand. It stung their faces and made them turn toward the forest.

Squid was crying.

The engine roared; the rotors thrashed at the air. They had to shout to hear each other.

"Better go!" said Murray.

Hannah told him: "You're coming."

"I can't." He hunched up his shoulders. "The light—"

"A replacement!" she shouted. "He could be here tomorrow."

He puckered his face against a hail of grit that swirled around them. He shook his head.

They had talked about it; they were all to go when the time came. Squid knew nothing of the city, of hospitals. She wanted her father along.

"Dad!" she cried.

"Sorry." He ducked his head. He put a hand on Hannah's shoulder, a hand on Squid's, and he pushed them toward that machine on the pad. The pilots were staring out through tinted glass, helmets on their heads. The side door was open, and a crewman beckoned in the downdraft.

Murray pushed harder. "Go!" he said. "Good luck!"

They ran out, Hannah and Squid. They ducked under the rotors, though the blades hammered round far above their heads. They threw their little bags inside and clambered up. Then the door swung shut, and the wind stopped on the instant, but inside the machine it was loud as thunder.

They were strapped into seats. The motor whined and the rotors chopped faster and faster. Then they tilted and rose backward into the sky. They pivoted past the trees, and Murray stepped out onto the pad. He leaned back his head and watched them go. And the pad, the forest, the whole island, twirled around him.

Squid was frightened. She sat in her seat stiff and pale, white like a pillar of salt. She had started all this, and it couldn't be stopped. And they flew off to face the ending alone.

She tapped at Hannah's shoulder. "Well, Mom," she said. "Now it's the *world* against the girls."

Hannah feels sorry for Murray. He's watching her like a lost little boy. Such hopes he had for this. The planning he did, for his daughter's return.

Squid stalks out onto the porch. She snaps open her purse, then lights a cigarette. She breathes out the smoke with a tremendous sigh.

"She smokes?" says Murray, deliberately quiet. Then

he smiles sadly. "Och, it must be hard on her, coming home like this."

Behind him, Tatiana is trapped on the stairs. She can't get by him, this big block of a man. She tries to scoot between his legs, but there isn't room. She can't climb to the rail. So she reaches out her doll and—ever so softly—touches its hand on the back of his leg. He smiles at her, and her face brightens.

Murray bends down. He picks her up with his hands under her arms. She's frightened by that, and drops the doll in her hurry to grab on to something.

Murray turns and puts her gently down. "There you go," he says. "There's the wee Tatty, safe on the floor."

She'll bolt, thinks Hannah. She'll go screaming through the door. But she doesn't. She stands right where Murray put her, her head tilted back so far that she almost topples over. She's grinning, or sort of grinning.

"And here's your dolly." He collects it from the floor and puts it in her hands. "There's your Barney doll."

She clutches it to her chest as a toddler would, shoulders thrust forward as she wriggles in excitement. Murray stares at Hannah over the child's head. "Can't she talk?" he asks.

Squid snorts. "Of course she can." She drops her cigarette on the porch and grinds it out on the fresh paint. "She doesn't, that's all. She never talks to people she doesn't know."

Tatiana holds up her hands toward Murray. He lifts her again, and she buries her face in the curve of his neck.

"I'll tell you what," he says. "I think it's time to see the new sandbox. You want to play in the sand, little Tat?"

She nods against his neck. "Hmm?" asks Murray.

"Forget it, Dad," says Squid.

But Murray's so stubborn. "What do you say? Would you like to do that?"

"Play me sandbox," says Tatiana.

And Squid looks nearly terrified.

chapter three

THEY FOLLOW THE PATHS, MURRAY IN FRONT, his boots leaving scuffs in the gravel. Hannah, behind him, sees the way the child fits in his arm, and she's struck for a moment with a powerful nostalgia.

She sees him carrying Squid down the same path, toward the white bulk of the tower. It's an image of absolute clarity, a picture from eons ago. It's so strong that it scares her. To go back to that part of her life, to live it all again, is a horror in her mind. She holds on to that child who's now a woman. She puts her arm tight around Squid's waist.

There's not a hint of fat, no need at all for a belt to keep the jeans in place. She slips a finger in through an empty loop and feels the denim moving stiffly in her hand. "I'm glad you've come," she says.

Squid sighs. "I wish Dad would say that."

"You know he never would," she says. "But he's happy too." And then she adds, "He told me so," a foolish lie.

"Sure." Squid drags her feet, stepping sideways just

enough to nudge Hannah's hand from her hip. "He's on at me already. Don't do this. Don't do that. It's like I never left."

Hannah nods. She wants to say, "Oh, just grow up!" But she daren't do that.

"I bet he blames me for what happened," says Squid. "I bet he thinks I killed Alastair."

"Oh, nonsense."

"But it was him, wasn't it? It was all Dad's fault what happened."

Hannah doesn't answer. Really, she thinks that's true.

⌒

Even Squid is delighted with the sandbox. She drops to her knees and plays with the toys, pushing the wooden *Darby* close against the lighthouse.

"Dad, this is great," says Squid. "It really is."

Murray sets Tatiana onto the sand, on her feet, with her little hand cupped over his wrist. "Go on," he says. "It's all for you, Tatiana."

He smiles at her, then backs away, and she reaches for him with both her hands.

"She wants you to stay," says Hannah.

"Och," he says. "I can't do that. There's supplies to put away, the weathers to do. You know how it is."

Hannah and Squid look at each other. "Work first, play after!" they shout in unison.

Murray grins. And for a moment it seems everything is just the way it used to be. Tatiana busies herself with the wooden ferry. She drives the cars down the ramp, then sits her doll on the empty deck. It rides atop the boat like a giantess.

"That's good, Tat," says Murray. "You give your Barney doll a ride." Then he stands and tugs his belt. "Right," he says. "I'm off then."

"Don't hurry," says Hannah. "And, Murray, don't carry too much at a time."

He answers with a wave of his hand, already on his way toward the tractor. Squid leans back, a look of fondness on her face, and Hannah sighs to see it. It has always surprised her how Squid can leap from one emotion to another, with the same ease that took her bounding down the beach along tangled piles of logs.

"I thought I'd die if he said that once more," says Squid. "Hasn't he ever heard of a Barbie doll?"

"How could he?" says Hannah. "You never had one. You never had a doll in your life."

"That doesn't mean I didn't want one." She shrugs. "I guess he was scared I would kill it." Then she rocks forward and makes a big show of getting to her feet. "Oh," she says, "I feel so old sometimes. Come on, Mom. I'll help you with the weathers."

"And what about Tatiana?"

"What about her?" she says. "When I was that age I was rowing a boat by myself."

It's an exaggeration, but not that much of one. "Independence," Murray liked to say. "The best thing you can do for a child is, really, nothing at all." He said it a lot, Hannah remembers now.

Squid takes one more minute at the sandbox. She parks the tiny wooden cars neatly at the edge. "Stay here," she tells Tatiana. "I won't be long, okay?"

Hannah walks half a step in front, along the path and

over the trestle. It dips down from each end to the middle, but even there it's thirty feet above the shards and crags of rock, the water torn to froth. But on winter days, with a southeaster blowing sixty knots, the surf rages wild, booming in the gap. Whole logs pinwheel on the waves and hammer at the wooden bridge, and no one—not even Murray—ventures from island to tower across it.

Squid slows at the middle, but doesn't stop. She says, "Mom, remember when—"

"I'll never forget," says Hannah.

Squid laughs, and hurries to come alongside.

Once, when Squid was young, Hannah found her dangling from the center of the bridge, hanging like a bat from her knees. She had a comb wrapped in tissue paper, and was humming through it. "Twinkle, Twinkle, Little Star." Hannah hauled her off. "Why on earth were you doing that?" she asked. "Because," said Squid, all of six years old, "Alastair said it couldn't be done."

Squid is still smiling as they trudge up the end of the bridge. She veers to her left toward the screen, the slatted white box of weather instruments.

"Don't bother with that," says Hannah.

"Why not? You have to do climats."

"Just twice a day now," says Hannah. "No one cares about humidities."

"Since when?" Squid's fingers hover at the latch.

"A while," says Hannah. "Oh, your father was angry. He said we might as well cut a hole in the front of that box and let the birds makes houses inside."

"I'll bet he did the climats anyway," says Squid.

Hannah laughs. It's true. Murray stuck to his old routine

until the Coast Guard men got rude. Then he told her, "Why don't they shut us down and cast us both in bronze? We're nothing but ornaments as it is."

In the whitewashed room at the tower's base, the scanner's on, voices chattering. Green Island is reporting northeast winds of twenty knots. Squid nods toward the speaker. "That doesn't sound like Mawson."

"It's not," says Hannah. She opens the barometer box and squints at the level. "Mawson left two years ago."

"He left?"

"Shhh!" Hannah always fumbles with the tables, the writing now so tiny.

"Sorry," says Squid, with a little grimace. She watches as Hannah adjusts the reading for temperature and elevation. The moment the box is shut she says, "I thought they'd be there forever."

"Well, so did he, I suppose," says Hannah.

"But *she* didn't think that way."

"No." She peers at the dial and writes the levels down: only ten knots now, but gusting still. The swell roars outside.

"Three-foot moderate," says Squid.

"I'll make it four." Hannah was always more cautious than Squid.

It's Triple Island's turn now on the circuit. Squid gives a little twinge at the gap that Hannah hardly catches anymore; Lucy and Lawyer have been missing from the reports for two years, both automated, their familiar voices lost forever, as though the islands themselves vanished in some tidal catastrophe. At times, Hannah thinks of the lights as folks in a rest home; one day another one's gone, and the others wonder who'll be the next.

"Who's at Triple?" asks Squid. "Anyone new?"

"No, he's still there," says Hannah, knowing it's Corrigan she's asking about. Squid used to stay after the weathers to chat with him on the ALAN circuit, the party line for keepers. They giggled and laughed, gushing fictional endearments just because they knew everyone was listening up and down the coast. It amuses Hannah to think there are still people on the lights who won't speak to Corrigan, shocked as they are by a romance between a middle-aged man and a girl not a third his age.

Now it's Lizzie's turn. Squid takes the handset from its cradle. She pushes the button, and talks.

"Who's that?" Her voice is unfamiliar at Coast Guard radio.

"It's Squid," she says. "Squid McCrae."

A babble of voices squawks from the speaker. She knows them all, old friends she recognizes only like a blind person—only by sound. Friends she sat up with on nights of screaming wind, when waves battered at tower walls and the spray—thick as snow—set automatic horns howling like lost souls. She sat with them on nights crackling with electrical storms, on days when tidal waves were zooming toward the islands at six hundred miles an hour. And on clear nights, too; on perfect nights, just to hear another voice in this huge and lonely blackness of the ocean.

All the voices come at once, bubbling with happiness and questions. Squid talks for a while, then abruptly passes the handset to Hannah. She jams it toward her, a sentence half finished, her lip quivering and her eyes blinking madly. And Hannah reads out the weathers over the sound of her daughter sobbing in the corner.

When she hangs up, she fiddles unnecessarily with the pencil and the book. Squid sniffles and gasps as the speaker drones on, through Bonilla and Langara and on to the south. And after the last one has reported, the circuit buzzes with this latest and exciting gossip. A voice new to the lights, not thinking who might hear, asks, "Wasn't she pregnant? Wasn't that the girl who went crazy?"

Squid lets out a stifled little cry. Then bolts through the door.

Hannah knows it's a silly fear. But for some weird reason she expects to find her daughter dangling head down from the bridge. And the truth, she sees, is nearly as bad.

Squid is folded up on a smooth shelf of rock, one of her childhood places, a stony love seat on a clifftop. She's got a handful of pebbles, and she's flinging them one by one into the sea. She says, accusingly, "What did you tell them?"

"Nothing," says Hannah. "You know I was with you. I—"

"Then what did *he* tell them?" A pebble hurtles down.

"Squid, that isn't fair." Just looking at that shelf of rock gives Hannah a feeling of spinning. "Your father wouldn't say a word. And you know that better than anybody."

Squid brushes the rest of her pebbles from her palm. They skitter down the rock face, leaping from the stone. In her silence she acknowledges that it's true about Murray. He would never talk about problems, or pains.

"It's only gossip," says Hannah. "You've seen how it works. The rumors spread *because* we kept it to ourselves."

"Well, my ears are still burning," says Squid. She shifts to the end of the hollowed seat, making room for her mother. But Hannah can't possibly join her, though it's only one step down from the grass. She sits instead at the top, as close as she dares to the edge.

"Mom?" says Squid. "Does Dad think I'm staying a long time?"

"He hopes you will. It's what he dreams about, that we're all together."

"All of us?"

"Yes. Alastair too."

Squid draws her legs up on the shelf. Hannah shivers; if she rolls sideways, she's gone. "Mom, does he dream that Alastair's still alive?"

Hannah has wondered that. She has seen him asleep in his chair, the old windup alarm ticking beside him, set to wake him for the weathers. She's seen, when he's sleeping, a smile on his face like none she's seen in years when he's awake. Sometimes he says his name, Alastair's name, and she never wakes him then. It would be too sad to see his face if he came awake thinking it was Alastair nudging his shoulder.

"Mom?" says Squid. "Do you ever wonder where Alastair is?"

"Sometimes," says Hannah. "Yes, sometimes I do."

"I see him in a library," says Squid. "A big quiet room full of dusty books, every book that was ever written. He just sits and reads. And he doesn't have to squint to see them."

"That's nice," says Hannah. "He'd be so happy there."

⌒

The *Darby* is going slowly down the channel as Hannah walks back with her daughter. The water lifts at its bow and curls back in a ripple. The smoke from the funnel thickens into swirls of brown and black.

Squid is watching it leave. By the way she slows as she walks, the way her head turns, Hannah wonders if she's wishing she were on it.

The whistle blows and they each raise a hand, the smallest of gestures. Hannah lets her scarf dangle down, swinging at her ankles.

Squid says, "I'm worried about Tat."

"Oh, you're doing all right," says Hannah. "She's a bit shy, that's all."

She feels she's spoken too quickly and somehow annoyed her daughter. Squid rolls her eyes. "That's not what I mean," she says.

"Then tell me."

It's almost there, an answer on her lips. But Squid simply stops on the path. "Oh my God," she says.

Hannah can't see what Squid has seen. Her eyes aren't as clear as they used to be.

"What is it?" she asks. "Squid, what's the matter?"

"A bird," says Squid. "A crow." She hurries along, and Hannah trots to keep up.

It's not a crow, but a raven. It's enormous—nearly half of Tatiana's size—its feathers unruly and ragged. It's perched on Murray's toy lighthouse, just a foot from her. But she seems oblivious to it, busy with the wooden cars and the chunky little ferry. If the bird stretched its wings it could touch her.

"Tatiana!" shouts Squid. But only the raven looks up. It twists on the top of the lighthouse with a sharp clatter of talons. And then, with no hurry at all, it spreads its wings and rises, with a melodic croak and a whistle of feathers, up to the roof and on to the sky.

The sand is pitted with tracks, with ruts and scraped-away hollows, as though a dozen birds had scuffed among the wooden boats. Hannah stares at the patterns of crosses and diamonds as Squid, kneeling down, starts to scrape them away. She does it almost frantically, and the grains rise up through her fingers; they flow past her hand to make wide sweeping fans. And Tatiana keeps playing, until Murray comes up, and she turns to look at him with a grin on her face.

"Hello, Tatty," he says. And then surely he sees the tracks that are left, for his head jerks back with surprise. "So." He smiles at Hannah. "We've another one like that."

She was thinking the same thing, remembering how the wild birds flocked around Alastair. They filled the trees, ravens next to gulls, cormorants with crows. They spaced themselves along the branches to hear the music that he played. And this raven from the sandbox might have joined them then. They live a human lifetime, Hannah knows. He might have been on Lizzie when Murray came to live here.

"It's not the same," says Squid. Her hand rubs at the

sand so hard that it squeaks. "One raven, that was all. It was picking for shells and fleas."

"Och," says Murray, with a shake of his head. "She's come home, Squid. Can't you see? She's come home."

He said those same words to Hannah the first time she met him. She was kayaking along the coast, from Vancouver to Alaska, in the days when very few would even think of doing that. Her boat was canvas over wood, her clothes just wool and cotton. For a girl alone, only nineteen, it was a thing of daring and adventure; she was like that once.

In Prince Rupert a fisherman told her, "Be sure to stop at Lizzie Island. It's like something from the Caribbean." He spoke of sandy beaches, a sheltered lagoon. His hands drew sweeping curves across the air. "And there's a lighthouse there," he said. "The keeper's like a hermit."

She paddled across the sound, from Tugwell bar to Melville Island, then through the gap below Dunira. And she saw the light then, Lizzie light. She thought it was cheerful and brave.

For three days she camped in the rain and waited for the wind to shift. The bugs came in clouds; they covered her tent and crawled through the wool of her sweaters. They blackened her skin like coal dust. And when the weather broke, late on the fourth day, she didn't give a thought for time or tides. She loaded her kayak and set off for Lizzie.

It was farther than she'd thought. Darkness came and the moon rose behind her. She paddled down a silvery path, toward the beacon that flickered on the wave tops.

She landed at two in the morning, in a hush of surf at the back of the island. She built a fire of salty wood that crackled and sparked, and she lay beside it, on her back, watching the stars.

In the morning the sun glinted off sand that was silver and gold. The surf broke in a continuous rumble, echoing back from the forest behind her, as though the island were breathing. She found old railway tracks buried in the sand, and followed them up to the crumpled ruins of a boat shed. There was a trail that took her over moss and devil's club, round windfalls and enormous old cedars, past tumbling banks of shells turned gray with age. Then a side trail led down to the shore, to a smooth shelf of rock where sea lions lay like buff-colored slugs, in a mass all over one another.

As she walked closer, one of them arched up from the rock, pushing with its flippers. Then the whole herd, with a ferocious bluster and roar, rushed headlong to the water. They tumbled and slid; they rolled from their shelves. They went in a wonderful, thundering rush, and the sound stirred the birds into a screaming cloud of white and black.

There was one animal left. It was a pink blob high on the rock. Then it stood up on freckled legs and snatched at a towel.

"You gave me a fright," he said, calling down. It was Murray McCrae.

He gathered his clothes and walked barefoot over the barnacles, as fast as he could, hopping and flouncing like a pink elf. He disappeared behind a boulder.

"Do you know," he said from there—half shouting—"that sea lions are the original mermaids?"

She saw an elbow, a knee, a flash of bright hair. "Really?" she said.

"When the sailors came across them—they must have been years at sea—they saw chubby and voluptuous women."

His voice was soft, his words almost like a song.

"Frankly, I don't see it myself," he said. "Imagine a woman like that, with arms but no legs." He came around the boulder in kneesocks and shorts. He was fitting the buttons into his shirt, but he had them in the wrong holes. "Och," he said. "She'd flop like a dying fish, a woman like that. But they're fascinating creatures, sea lions. Do you know that the bulls collect whole harems of females?"

And then he blushed.

Later, Hannah would see the same thing, a rambling babble, from other men who spent years alone on the lights. But at the time, she thought Murray McCrae was just plain odd.

"What's your name?" he asked.

"Hannah James," she said. The first words that she'd spoken.

"I'm Mr. McCrae," he told her. "Hannah, have you ever seen a lighthouse?"

He took her on what he called the grand tour. He showed her everything, talking all the time. He took her to the powerhouse and pointed out the parts of the generator as it rumbled away in its spotless house. "The injectors here; one, two, three, four of them." He had to shout to make himself heard. "The starter motor, see. Twelve-volt, of course. It's a three-phase generator, pumping out a hundred and ten volts." He stepped back, then looked around the room. "What else?" he asked. "Oh, yes. Silly me." And he unscrewed a battery cap, to let her see the acid.

"And now," he said. "The tower."

She loved the tower, its staircase spiraling up, the huge lantern with the polished machine in the middle, the prism and lens turning slowly around. "Don't look right at it," he warned. "It would burn your eyes in an instant."

When they stepped out to the platform he was talking less quickly, more carefully, and his voice had lost its shrill of excitement. They stood in the sunshine, looking at the island.

He had been there nearly ten years already. He was a coal miner's son, from Drumheller, Alberta. "I was lucky," he said. "Sheer blind luck. I went looking for a job the day after the lightkeeper died. They were desperate for a replacement."

"What happened to him?" asked Hannah.

"Oh," said Murray. He looked away. "I believe that he died here on the island."

The house was nearly empty. Murray had burned all the old, moldering furniture the previous winter and was now building his own a piece at a time, starting with whole logs pulled from the beach. He had one chair and no table, but a wallful of shelves full of books. Hannah stared at the titles, standing before them with her hands at her back, as he boiled crabs for their dinner.

"Are you a biologist?" she called to the kitchen. There were books about plants, books about animals. There wasn't a novel among them.

"No," he shouted back.

She waited for more, but it was all he said.

They sat on the floor to eat, cracking the shells with their hands, using the crabs' pointed feet to dig out the flesh from the claws. It was just before dark when they walked back down the trail to the camp.

Hannah had heaped sand onto the fire, and the coals were hot underneath. They stoked them with moss-covered twigs and slivers of cedar that Murray peeled from a log with his little red knife. Then he fanned up flames with a copy of the Audubon guide that he carried in his pocket the way her own father had once carried the Book of Common Prayer.

She was smitten with Murray. He was a gentle, shy man who hadn't touched so much as her elbow. He was twice her age and a little more, and she found that exciting. But dangerous too.

"Sit with me," said Hannah. She spread her poncho on the sand. She didn't bother unfolding it first. "Come on," she said, and patted the cloth, quartered into a square.

Murray sat in the sand.

He wasn't about to seduce her. And she sighed and thought it was all for the best. In the morning she would load up her kayak and paddle away to the north. But then the auklets came; it was the auklets that kept her on Lizzie.

It got very dark. She watched Murray prod at the fire. And then she heard a whistling, and something darted past her head. It crashed through the bushes behind her, crackling through the branches. Another came behind it.

"What was that?" she said, startled.

Murray poked at the fire. "Auklets," he said.

"They scared me," she told him.

Murray came beside her. She thought he was about to hold her, but he only reached past—"Excuse me," he said—and picked up his Audubon book. Two more of the things hurtled by with the same weird hum and whistle.

"Rhinocerous auklets," said Murray. He opened the

book and held it flat to the firelight. Hannah saw a funny, fat-bellied bird with a little spike of feathers above its beak.

"They feed far from shore," he said. "They come back after dark to their burrows in the woods."

Hannah had seen the holes; she'd thought they were marten dens.

The auklets came in a flurry, smashing blindly into the dry undergrowth.

"Och, for heaven's sake," said Murray. He was looking at the book, bending so close to the fire that Hannah worried he might set his hair alight. "They're not auklets at all. They're actually a type of parrot, if you can believe that."

"A parrot?" she said.

He twisted the book. Then he laughed. It was the first time she had heard his laughter, and it was a lovely sound. He said, "I can't read in this light. It says *puffin*. 'A type of parrot-billed puffin.' You see, I transposed the words."

Three or four auklets whirred past in the darkness. A straggler came blundering by, and then it was quiet.

"Apparently," said Murray, "they have very poor eyesight." He closed his book.

"But they find the island," said Hannah. "And I'm sure there's a hundred burrows back there, but each bird must go right to its house. How do they do that?"

The book cracked open. Murray hummed as he read. "It doesn't say." He slapped it against his palm. "What a question," he said. "What a puzzle. I think tomorrow I'll have to sleep out in the bushes here. Try to watch the burrows." He nodded. "I'll see if there's any coming and going."

He stood up then. The sand was cold and dewy, and it

stuck in a black patch to the seat of his shorts. "Well, good night," he said.

"Wait," she said. "Do you think . . ." He turned around. "Could I get a job here?" she asked. "Do you need an assistant or something?"

Murray stared at her. He said, "I think you belong here, Hannah James. Och, you've come home."

Squid is furious. "What do you mean she's come home?" she asks. "She hasn't come home at all." She whisks Tatiana from the sandbox. Grains whirl in the sun like shaken salt. "She's never been here before, so don't say she's come home."

Murray shrinks into sadness. "I only meant," he says, "that she's so much like family."

"Family?" says Squid. Hannah, too, is shocked by the rage. Squid is shaking. "She doesn't look like you. She's never met you."

"Well, she's family now," says Murray. It amazes Hannah that he can go patiently, doggedly on. "I don't give a fig about anything else."

Squid laughs her ugly laugh. "You sure did," she says. "When it happened." She rears back. From her forehead to her neckline she's a vivid red. "Well, guess what?" she cries.

"Stop it!" shouts Hannah. "The two of you stop it!" She lunges between them, frantic to keep them from opening doors that aren't meant to be opened. She can almost imagine a squeal of old hinges, the echo of voices down cobwebbed corridors. It's Squid's fault, she thinks;

Squid has always done this. She's the only McCrae who'll go rampaging through these private and secret places.

Hannah shakes her finger, first at Squid and then at Murray. It horrifies her that she is actually shaking a finger under Murray's nose. "And now," she says, another echo from the past, "not another word from either of you."

Murray looks shocked; absolutely shocked. His pale eyebrows arch on a sunburned forehead. Squid laughs. Surprisingly, Tat does too—a glimmer of life dancing in her eyes.

Hannah forces her face into a look that's meant to seem stern. Already, she can see, the matter is settled as far as Squid is concerned. Squid can forget these things, these arguments, as easily as she can shrug her shoulders. It's not the same, though, for Murray.

Squid lifts Tatiana onto the grass. "I guess I'll get settled in," she says, and passes between her parents, off across the grass.

Murray looks down at his sandbox, at the weave of bird tracks. "Och," he says, with a sigh. Then, louder: "Tat! You forgot your Barney doll!"

"Are you going to let her stay in the small house?" asks Hannah.

He says, "She might as well do what she wants. It's what she'll do at any rate." And again his words are an echo from the past.

By the middle of July, her first year on the island, Hannah was sharing the big house with Murray. They didn't share a bed; there wasn't one yet. They slept on a fat bolster stuffed with sphagnum moss. They made love only when the sun went down, when the room was so dark that Murray could undress without her seeing.

The summer days were long. It was September before Hannah was pregnant. She was twenty years old. She wanted their child to be born on the island.

Murray shivered and shook through April and May, afraid he would faint when he was needed the most. He had a vision that he would keel over headfirst into the barrel-shaped baby bath, and drown as Hannah flopped on the bed like a mermaid. But he did just fine. He delivered the baby, then hovered so close that Hannah got frightened; she thought he had snared himself in the umbilical cord.

Squid came along a year later, a year and a day, on a night that was stormy. They named her Elizabeth, after the island. She wasn't expected for another month; like everything she'd do in the years ahead, she surprised her parents that night. There was blood and pain, an anguished scream, and the wind howled and shook at the walls.

It was sooner than they'd planned, but already they had the two children they'd hoped for. "And now," said Murray, with great earnestness, "it's clear sailing from here."

In December of that year, a week before Christmas, a mission boat stopped at the island. It had come from Lawyer and was off to Langara, taking Santa Claus to the lighthouse children. Murray and Hannah were married in the boat's little chapel as it rocked in a swell from the west. Their witness was Santa Claus, standing beside them with his beard off, twirling it between his fingers.

That night, their wedding night, Murray told her, "If

the children ever ask, we were married two years sooner. Is that all right with you?"

They never asked, though they could have by the time they were two, so quickly did they grow and age. Before they could walk, they could swim. Murray wanted it that way. He taught Alastair; Hannah taught Elizabeth, who—typically—developed her own style, more like a beetle than anything else. She could swim backward as fast as she could going ahead, squirting along under the surface with punches and kicks. "We've got ourselves a squid," said Murray. And the name stuck like glue.

"Maybe you should teach her how to really swim," Hannah said. But Murray saw no point in that.

"You might as well let her do what she wants," he said. "It's what she'll do at any rate."

⁓

Murray opens the legs of the Barbie like a pair of scissors. He sits it in the sand, its arms reaching stiffly forward. To Hannah, it looks like a ridiculous shrunken woman asking to be picked up. Murray stoops again, and folds its arms to its sides.

"She looks like you," he says. "Don't you think? A little bit?"

Hannah knows right away he's not comparing her to the Barbie doll. He's talking about Tatiana. This is his way; he analyzes conversations.

"Squid seems angry with me," he says. "I don't know why." Then again he bends the doll, stretching it flat in the sand. Finally he's satisfied, and he stands up. "Why is that, Hannah?"

She touches his arm. "I think her plans aren't working out."

"What plans are those, then?"

Hannah doesn't know; she can only guess. "I think she's having troubles with Tatiana." The child is like a moon snail, sealed up in a hard and shuffling shell. Hannah can't imagine Tatiana having friends. She can't see her lasting a single day in any sort of school. "I think that Squid might want our help."

"A first time for everything," says Murray. But he dwells on this, too, as they walk toward the big house. The sun has moved behind the tower; a shadowy finger lies stretched on the grass. In a few hours the beacon will be stronger than the sun, and the top of the shadow, the lantern, will flicker in the flashing of the light.

"Och, I still don't see it," says Murray. "If she wants our help why doesn't she ask?"

"Maybe she's waiting to be told."

"And who'll do that, then?" Murray grimaces. "Who'll take the first poke at the tiger?"

"Oh, Murray."

"Och, I suppose she's only upset. She comes home and everything's changed."

Changed? Hannah nearly laughs. *What can change?* she wants to ask, but doesn't. The island never will; Murray never will. As far as Squid could possibly know, not a single thing has changed.

She lays her scarf across her shoulders and sways against Murray as they walk along. He's still thinking, still brooding, but he surprises her with what he asks next.

"Do you ever wonder," he says, "if the old keeper had any children?"

⁓

Murray didn't tell her that first day that the old keeper had hanged himself. For eight days or more his body dangled from the tower, swaying in autumn winds with a bit of rope around his neck. The sun rose on him and set again; it rose and set as he twirled slowly round in a big old oil-skin coat as black as death. And she'd sat there with Murray in the very same place.

It was Squid who saw the keeper first. She was only five years old. On a night of electrical storms, she looked up and saw him there. "There's a man on the tower," she said, matter-of-fact, and Murray went terribly pale.

And then Hannah saw him too, on a misty, sultry morning. He stood staring out to sea, and then he turned to look at her. And he vanished in a swirl of fog.

"So you're one of those," said Murray.

"One of what?" she asked.

"A ghost seer. Not everyone sees ghosts, you know."

⁓

Murray doesn't walk with her all the way to the house. He veers off instead toward his favorite place. He'll change the oil in the number three engine, the one that never runs. Then he'll sit for a while in the warm, diesely rumble of the powerhouse. Hannah thinks of it as his little womb, a place for him to think.

He leaves her by the steps. The wind is easing off, the

sea is dropping. She can still hear the surf, if she listens, but it's less of a roar now. By nightfall, the wind sock will sag from its pole like a flaccid old condom. The gulls will settle in the channel like rows of net floats. The auklets will come hurtling home.

Hannah stands alone. In a month at most the winds will shift to the south. Then the gray whales will pass the island on their southward way to Mexico. The humpbacks will go off on their journey to Hawaii, and the birds will pass in the thousands. The Undertaker will come, and Hannah will be off on her way.

She can't stand it anymore, winter on the island. Days eight hours long, endless nights crammed with Murray into a brooding, shrunken world. The storms, one after another. The rain. And worse, her fear of the snow.

It's a secret that she'll keep from Squid: She hasn't spent a winter on the island for three years. Since her daughter fled, Hannah hasn't lived on Lizzie for more than five months at a stretch. She comes and goes—like an auklet, she thinks—struggling blindly to find a home. But if this is what Murray meant by everything changing, it's the first time he's ever said a word about it.

chapter four

ALASTAIR'S ROOM SMELLS CLEAN AND fresh. It's dusted and polished and perfect. His books are set precisely on the shelves, every one as straight as a soldier. The afghan, with its weird Maltese patterns that change from shapes into people and back into shapes, might be a drum skin stretched on his bed. But along one wall are cockeyed, twisted shelves, nearly the only thing in the world that he made for himself.

It isn't a sad place, as Squid had thought it might be. Really, it feels no different than it ever did, as though Alastair—at any moment—might come suddenly up the stairs and find her here again.

"Why don't you just give up?" he asked her, the last time.

He startled her that day. She felt her heart leap, her shoulders tighten, and she almost screamed, but didn't. She kept her back toward him as he went to sit in the window seat, beside the closet door.

"I told you," he said. "It's not in the closet."

"I didn't look in your closet," she said, trying to sound affronted.

"Then how did this piece of paper fall off the top of the door?"

He reached down from his chair and picked up a tiny piece of folded yellow paper. The light from the window glared on his glasses. It made them opaque, as pale as his skin, as though underneath he had no eyes at all.

"You're nuts," she said. "You know that, Alastair? You're crazy as a bug."

He laughed. It was the last time she ever heard him laugh. He said, "Now where would I put it? What a problem that is. What a knotty little problem."

He looked like a professor, like a mad scientist, his head bulging above the glasses, the hair that he never combed all clotted into spikes and wads.

He said, "You can look as long as you want, Squid. But it will be doomsday when you find it."

～

She sits on the bed and touches the things on the shelf, but so gently that they don't even move from their places. She stares at the map that he made as a child, reading the silly names they'd invented together.

He did everything so seriously. He learned from his father the importance of work, the sense of duty above everything else. Even as children, it seems to Squid, they worked like slaves at the lightkeeping tasks, the endless chores of painting and rust chipping, of weeding and planting, that had to be finished to Murray's exactness before he would spare a moment or two for anything like pleasure.

"Work first, play after." That was the rule they lived by. And it made Alastair what he was; it doomed him to a lonely, frustrated life.

She takes the map in her hands. It has been folded and unfolded many times. Its edges are brittle where the salt water soaked it and dried. Some of the writing is smudged.

It was raining that day.

They stood at the edge of the water, the boat on the beach and all their belongings beside it. Murray had brought a load of things down with the tractor.

"Just remember," he said. "There's nothing there that can hurt you. There's no beasties or monsters. You'll see nothing at night you don't see in the day."

"Oh, yes we will," said Alastair. He was eight years old; his birthday had passed just a month before. He didn't wear glasses yet, but he squinted a lot. "The auklets aren't there in the daytime, Dad. The rock beetles only come out in the night."

"Well, you know what I mean," said Murray. "Don't be scared just because it's dark."

"I won't!" cried Squid. She remembers now the way she said it, the way Murray smiled when she put her hand against her hip. "I've got this!" she said, and touched the knife in its leather pouch. "And if anything comes after us I'll slash it into bits!"

"Good girl!" said Murray. "And you've got your life jackets too?"

Alastair nodded.

"Then I'll be off," said Murray.

"Dad," Alastair called after him. "You won't be worried, will you?"

"Of course not," he said. "You're on your own, the pair of you. The best thing a parent can do for a child is—"

"Really, nothing at all!" cried Alastair and Squid together.

Murray beamed. "I'll see you tomorrow," he said, and went off on the tractor.

They loaded the boat with all their gear. They filled it so full they had to wait for the tide to come in and float it off the beach. Alastair sat ready at the oars, sweeping them over the sand now and then as the water filled in around them. "Get out and push," he said.

There was nothing she wouldn't do for Alastair.

⌒

She turns from the bed at the sound of squeaking floors. Tatiana is there, her thumb in her mouth, a finger crooked over her nose.

"Hey," says Squid. "I thought you were sleeping."

The child stares at her with huge, wondering eyes.

"Lonely?" No answer. "You want to sleep in here? You want to lie down beside Mom?"

Squid pats the afghan, but Tatiana comes only as far as Alastair's mat. She plops to the floor on the braided rope, falling backward with her knees stiff. Her thumb pops from her mouth like a cork, but she puts it back, blinks at Squid, then settles down on her side.

"There you go. I used to lie there myself sometimes."

Squid goes back to the map, holding it nearly flat, staring at the drawings Alastair made—the landforms—as though by turning them sideways she might see the islands rising from the paper sea.

The big one sprawls across the middle, every curve of beach precisely drawn. The outer islands are just the same, but only on the sides that face the big one. At the time, they were moons, with just one face familiar, and all the rest a mystery. The backs of them, on the map, are sketched in faint and cautious lines.

He climbed the tower to draw it. Of course she went with him, to pass him the pencils and eraser as he commanded, to call out the bearings from the handheld compass that he couldn't quite read when it was right before his eyes. They drew a world with the tower right at the center.

"When we finish this," said Alastair, "we'll go exploring, and we'll discover the islands. We'll name them, every one."

"Why don't we name them from here?" she asked.

"You have to land on them to name them," he said. "That's the way it works."

"Then why do we need a map?" she said.

"So we know where we're going."

It didn't make sense to her. Only Alastair could understand. He had the map held down on a clipboard that he leaned against the railing. His tongue came out from his mouth as he drew.

"Take a bearing," he said, "on that island there."

"Which one?"

He pointed. "That one, Squid."

"You mean North Island?"

"Oh, Jiminy, Squid," he said, sounding just like Murray. "It's not called North Island. Not until we get there."

He drew every bit of land that he could see, with lovely squiggles for the shore. And the farther he got from the tower, the more his lines grew faint, until they faded away into nothing. He drew great slashes at the edges. "Reefs," he wrote to the north. At the south, "Here there be rocks."

"You mean here there *are* rocks," she said.

He told her, "You wouldn't understand."

And the next day they set off, in Murray's glass-bottomed boat. They hoisted a broomstick and flew a flag that Alastair made, a little red cross on a square of white. He said, "We'll plant that flag and claim all the land for ourselves."

It seems so silly now, though at the time it was such an adventure. A *mission*, Alastair called it. "You can be captain," he said, and wasn't she proud of that? Until he told her, "*I'll* be the admiral, and the navigator."

Tatiana's not quite asleep, but nearly. Her eyes open and close as she watches her mother. She's small and fragile, and Squid can't imagine letting her go wandering off alone in a boat, without a thought for her safety.

But Hannah didn't even bother to see them away.

They went alone, like Columbus did, proud at the time of their independence. But now it seems sad to Squid. She wonders sometimes if she was ever truly loved.

She smiles at her daughter. "Okay, Tatiana?"

The map is covered with names. Most of them are ridiculous, written in all sizes of letters. "BlAck sKulL ISLaNd." "BiG RocK rOCk." "CaMPfIre PoinT." Squid is embarrassed to see them now, in her own pathetic writing. Only one of the names ever came into use; the little rocky island with its group of huddled cedar trees, the place that would become Alastair's refuge, was called Almost Nothing Atoll.

Squid lays the paper back on the bed. She looks up at the shelves crowded with books, along the bent and twisted ones, down to the bureau with a microscope on top, searching for a strip of red.

Alastair started his notebook that day. He used it to record the times they arrived on each island, the interesting things they found. It was only later that he used it for a journal. And then he was so secret about it that she didn't even know he was doing it until weeks before his death.

"What are you writing?" she asked, surprising him at his desk.

"Nothing," he said.

"Let me see."

He was so sad then. He was skinny and pale. He folded himself over top of the book, shielding it with his arms and his chest. "It's private," he said.

"You let me look before." She walked up and stood beside him. "You showed it to me all the time."

"That was years ago," he said. His glasses slid from his nose and hit with a thud on the desk. They stood on their lenses, rocking softly, magnifying ovals of the wood.

"Come on," she said. "Please, Alastair?"

His eyes were puffy and pale, so strange that she realized she hadn't seen him once without his glasses in at least a year or more. There was a huge bright welt across his nose. "Leave me alone," he said.

"Are you writing about me?"

His whole face turned as red as the welt. "I write about *things*," he said. "About stuff."

"I want to see."

She tried to force her arms under his. He fought against her. He pushed her away and slammed the book shut. He leaned his elbows on it, his pointed spikes of elbows. And then he collapsed; he started to cry. "It's private," he said again. "Let me have *something* on this island that's just my own."

"Okay," she said.

"Please promise me that."

"I promise," she said.

Still, he didn't trust her. He hid the book, and it took her nearly half an hour to find it, tucked where it was behind the others on the shelf, standing up against the back of the bookcase. She took it to her own room and sat with her shoulders against the closed door. And she went first to the last thing he'd written.

I'm drowning. Can't breathe, can't surface, can't escape. Dad just WILL NOT LISTEN!!!! Mom can't persuade him and won't even try anymore. Thank God for Squid. It would be HELL here if it wasn't for Squid. I'm afraid to tell her that I think I'm

The page ended there, and she didn't turn it. She closed the book, feeling dirty and ashamed. She felt just the way she had the time Murray found her sunbathing naked on the back porch of Gomorrah, feet together, arms spread wide across the hot red paint. She touched the book to her forehead; she rapped it on her brow.

But the book had a power. It called to her like a siren to a sailor, tempting her with all its secrets. She felt that she would not be able to set it down; it would cling like tar to her fingers. Or if she could, it would only leap again into her hands. She couldn't possibly *not* find out what Alastair was too frightened to tell her.

I think I'm going blind.

I think I'm going insane.

She cracked open the book; her finger still marked the right place. She wanted to see that one sentence and no other. No matter what it said, she would not read any more.

Alastair's letters slanted backward. They leapt over the page with no thought for the lines. They shouted at her, full of rage and frustration.

I'm afraid to tell her that I think I'm

She plucked at the edge of the page, peeling back the corner. And suddenly she hurled the book away. It hit the wall and fluttered down like a wounded bird. It crumpled on the floor, upright with the pages fanned toward her. And she sat, and she stared at the thing; she couldn't betray him that way.

In her whole life she'd met no more than fifty people. But no one on earth could have a greater sense of righteousness than Alastair. "I have a rule," he'd told her.

"Don't do something if there's a single person—anywhere—that you don't want to know what you're doing."

She collected the book, and she put it back where she found it. She was sitting downstairs when Alastair came in from the rain. He hung up his slicker. "What's the matter?" he asked.

"Nothing," she said. And then, hoping to make him smile, "Really, nothing at all."

He never smiled anymore. He frowned at her as he took off his glasses and wiped the rain from the lenses. He went upstairs. And a moment later he was back, storming down the steps, waving the book in his hand.

"You read it!" he said. "I asked you and asked you, and you went in and read it."

"I didn't," she said.

"You did!" He was whining. He trembled like a whirligig man. "I put a hair between the pages. And now it's gone. And there's no one on this whole stupid island who would do this except for you."

"You put a hair in there?" she said. "You're a nut, Alastair."

"Don't turn it onto me," he said. "You went through my room, and you found the book and you read it."

"I can't believe it." She shook her head. Inside, she felt awful, like an apple rotted below the skin. She looked at the ceiling and sighed. "He put a hair between the pages. What sort of a mind would think of that?"

Alastair breathed through his nose, a whistle and rasp. His hair stood up in tufts, and water dripped from the bony point of his chin. He sort of shrank inside himself, like a fan folding closed. "How could you do this?" he asked. "I trusted you, Squid."

"You did not," she said with a laugh. "You hid it away at the back of the shelves. And anyway . . ." She stood up. "I *didn't* read it, so you don't have to torture yourself. I found it, but I couldn't read it."

He didn't believe her, not fully. And she knew there was nothing more to say. She went out in the rain, and Alastair went back to his room. He turned the radio on and set the volume as high as he could. They only got the one station, the public broadcasting, and the house shook with the sound of opera. The deep voice of a tenor vibrated in the windows and the walls as Alastair, with a hammering and a screeching of nails, hid his book in a new place, one she would never find in all the hours that she looked.

Night after night she lay awake, reliving that moment when she fumbled through the shelves and found his book behind the others. She was haunted by his secret, but couldn't ask him what it was. And she wasn't fully sure that she didn't already know it.

I'm afraid to tell her that I think I'm

In her imaginings, a parade of nightmares passed before her.

I think I'm going to run away.

I think I'm going to murder them.

I think I'm going to kill myself.

Even now, more than four years later, Squid regrets what she did. She's sorry that she ever looked at the diary, but she's more sorry that she didn't read what her brother had written. She can't help thinking that she might have saved him if she had.

Oh, she tried to get it out of him. She asked him, "Alastair, dear. Is there something you'd like to tell me?"

"Like what?" he said. "What sort of thing?"

"I don't know." She shrugged. They were painting—on the house or tower, she can't remember which. Whatever it was, she was dangling in a bosun's chair as Alastair peered down from the top; he liked heights even less than his mother. Whatever it was, it was red or white, the only colors they ever saw inside a can of paint, and it was one of the last jobs they ever did together.

"Well, give me a clue," he said.

"Anything." She skittered sideways with her feet. She loved to hang in the bosun's chair. "You know. Stuff. Anything you'd like to say."

"Not really," he said. "Nothing you don't already know."

She pushed herself out and bounced back to the wall. Her shadow bounded beside her, meeting at her feet.

"Don't do that," said Alastair. "You're making me dizzy."

She did it all the harder. Her legs for springs, she shot herself back and forth, out so far that she twirled around before swinging in again. She felt the air rush against her back, then against her chest, against her bare legs, brown as hemlocks in their sawed-off denim shorts. The rocks and sky and grass went spinning past, and she laughed at the freedom she felt. But Alastair was horrified. "I can't watch," he said. "Oh, Jiminy, Squid. You're scaring me sick up here."

She pushed with her feet. She spun in the air. And she saw Murray below her, his head tilted up, his hands on his hips.

"Are you daft?" he shouted. "Stop that, before you break your damned neck."

She hit the wall with one foot and bounced off at an angle. Her back slammed against the wall.

"I've got hooligans for children," said Murray. "Alastair, I'm ashamed of you. Jiminy! Is your head full of sand?"

Squid stared at him, down between her legs. "It wasn't Alastair," she said. "Don't shout at Alastair."

"And why not?" he said. He crossed his arms. "You put the reins on the head of a horse, not on its arse."

And he wandered away. She saw the sun glinting in his hair as he shook his head again and again.

"You see?" said Alastair. "*Now* do you see what I mean?"

"What?" she asked.

"Why I feel like I'm drowning?"

―⁓―

Tatiana never closes her eyes when she sleeps. There's always a crack at the bottom, wider than the lashes, where the white shows through. Squid has sometimes seen the eyes moving, rapidly back and forth. She finds it a little spooky.

The child is using a hand for a pillow, her body curved along the whorls of the rope mat. Squid moves beside her; she slips her finger into Tatiana's fist. It pleases her to think that Alastair would like this, to see the girl asleep on his treasured creation.

It's soft rope, almost woolly, that once worked a fishing net in Dixon Entrance. Alastair found it cast up on the beach after a northerly gale, fifty fathoms of it nearly, tangled round the rocks and in among the driftwood. It took him two days to work it free, patiently pulling the whole length clear of every snag. He dragged it home in a long and twisting line, all his weight leaning forward to keep it moving on the boardwalk. He came back as proud as a hunter, as though pulling a monstrous snake that he'd slain.

"I'm going to make a mat," he said, and set to the job with that infuriating patience, puzzling out a sense from a terrible snare of half-closed loops and the intricate patterns of his knot. "It's basically a Turk's head," he told her, pushing up his glasses.

She said, "It looks like a ball of giant lint."

"Well, now it might," he said. "But when it's finished it'll be all flattened out."

She runs her fingers along the strands. They go over and under, around and around; she has no idea where he started, no idea where he stopped.

What a knotty little problem.

"Tat!" she says, jumping up. "Tat, wake up!" she shouts.

Tatiana, startled from her sleep, struggles on the mat. Squid hauls her up, laughing, and turns in a circle with the child in her arms. "Oh, Tat, you found it," she says, and sets her on the floor again. "You found it. You showed me right where it is."

She grabs the edge of the mat. The rope bunches in her fist. She lifts and shakes, and a shower of grit and sand goes tumbling down. The mat is heavy, and the edges fold under themselves as she drags it aside. Strands of the rope stretch and pop, and an oval of pale, dull floor appears, where the head of one nail stands like a stud, catching a long white thread.

Squid lets the mat fall with a whoosh of air. She stamps her heel on the bare patch of floor, on one board and then another, on a third and a fourth, until one of them chatters under her foot. She drops to her knees. She pries it up, her red-painted nails scratching at the wood. It lifts and falls back, then lifts again, and flips onto the floor with a smack. She hunches forward and peers into the space. There's not the one book she'd imagined, but eight. They disappear into the hole as far as her fingers can reach, all identical, bindings of red tape on dark blue covers. Tatiana crawls quietly beside her and stops at the edge of the hole.

"Listen," says Squid. "This is a secret, okay? We won't tell anyone about it. Not your grandpa. Not anyone."

Tatiana shakes her head.

"It's our little secret, just yours and mine."

She lifts four books at once. The edges are sticky with spiderwebs, the pages a deep yellow down at the bottom, nearly white at the top. They have a curious odor of dryness and age.

She puts them down at the edge of the oval left by the mat. She starts to put the floorboard back in place. But again the books have a power, and she leaves the hole gaping as she takes up one of the diaries.

February 10. *The* Darby *came. It brought books. Southward's* Grazing in Terrestrial and Marine Environments. *Elton's*

The Ecology of Invasions by Animals and Plants. *No sign of Ecological Monographs. Dad said it might come next week on the Sikorsky. I think he forgot to ask for it.*

Elton is fascinating. I think now that limpets are like herds of buffalo. They just wander along grazing all day. I think they have a sense of where they want to go and they seem to know the best places. I saw them come across the empty shell of a dead one and they seemed to gather round it and nudge at it. Dad says they were probably eating algae off the shell but I think they maybe know what death is and were trying to recognize an individual that used to travel with them.

February 11. *I tried to get Squid interested in limpets but she only laughed and went away. There's something wrong with my eyes. Things get blurry and out of focus, and my glasses don't seem to help. Dad says not to worry. He says I'm just a bit tired.*

Squid flips through the pages, forward and back.

February 12. *Dear God, please don't let me go blind. I know I don't pray very much and I don't think of you at Christmas but I'm frightened, God, and if you can do this I'll believe in you then. Please, please fix my eyes and let me look at all the wonderful things you made. I beg you for this please, God. Amen.*

February 14. *Squid seems restless. She's surly and snappy but I don't know why. She threw a paintbrush at me and called me a freak. Paint in my hair.*

She remembers that day. They were painting a fuel tank, and he kept moving the paint out of her reach, shifting the pail, leaving white rings interlocked in a line down the pad. They were talking about ravens. All that morning the birds had been soaring along the cliff, riding a wind that rose up the rock and carried them high in an instant. Wings held open, they did barrel rolls and loops.

"They're showing off," said Alastair. "They're trying to see which one's the best."

"Yeah, because the best one gets the girl," she said. "All they're doing is mating."

"No, it isn't that." He moved the pot and dipped his brush. He squinted as he painted.

"Sure," she said. "They can't conk each other on the head, so they fly around a bit."

She gazed at the sky. The ravens moved as fast as darts, soaring on the rising wind. "I wish I could do that," she said. "What a waste that only birds can fly."

"Just paint," he said. "Okay?"

"Don't you think it's a waste, Alastair?"

"No," he said, with a sigh. "Now let's get this done."

"But they're just machines. Little flying machines. They don't think about it. They just do it; they're birds."

She reached for the pail, but it was gone again. Alastair was staring at her. He said, "Do you mean that?"

"Yes, Alastair dear. They're birds. They really are."

"But you said they don't think. What do you mean they don't think?"

"What's to think about if you're a bird?" She watched him dip his brush again and spread another swath over paint that was already thick and sparkling white. The tank was painted every spring and every fall, according to Murray's schedule. "You fly, you eat, you poop a lot."

"Oh no," he said. "No. You fly up as high as you can, just to see what things look like from there. You go hurtling down and you think, I'll loop the loop when I get to the bottom. I'll do a roll and a spin, and I'll do it better than anyone else. You figure out where the clams are and how to break the shells. And when the sun goes down you think about tomorrow and all the things you'll do in the morning."

She laughed. "You sound like Dad."

"Paint!" he told her.

"Yes, *sir!*" she said. "Forget the dumb birds."

"They're not dumb," he said. "Ravens are smart. They've got the same IQ as a dog."

"As if you would know," she snorted.

"I do know." He slapped his brush against the steel. "I've read it in books. Lots of books."

"How many were written by birds?"

"That's stupid," he said.

"*You're* stupid." She turned to face him. "Your head's full of all these weird ideas, and when you get off this is-land what's going to happen then? Everyone's going to think you're a freak."

He turned his head as though she'd slapped him. His cheek was crimson, his pointed chin poking at his shirt.

"And you know what?" she cried. "You already are. You're a freak, Alastair."

He didn't look up; he didn't speak. He dabbed at the tank, and the paint dribbled down like tears.

"You've never kissed a girl; you've never ridden in an elevator. You've never played a baseball game and never watched TV. And in all your life you've never been more than thirty miles from home."

He answered in a childish voice. "What you say is what you are," he said. And she hit him with the brush.

She threw it hard; it went spinning from her hand. It spun in a blur, the red of the handle and the white of the bristles, flinging drops of paint. It smacked on the back of Alastair's head and ricocheted onto the grass. And still he didn't look up. He flinched when it hit him, then went on painting. There was a streak of white in his hair, a spray of white across the green of lawn.

Squid turned and sprinted off. She ran across the grass, past the whirligigs, past Gomorrah, down through the forest on the humps of the boardwalk. And she slowed to a walk when the futility struck her; she could only run in a circle and get back where she'd started.

It was true. She *was* a freak. They were all freaks, every one. But what difference would it make, so long as they stayed together? They *had* to stay together, but Alastair was desperate to be gone.

chapter five

IN THE KITCHEN OF THE BIG HOUSE, HANNAH unpacks the boxes as Murray brings them in. She is fondling the fresh crisp lettuce, gloating over tomatoes. It's been nearly a month since she held a banana, and she squeezes one gently. She holds it like a mustache below her nose to smell the smell of bananas.

The back door opens again. Murray kicks off his shoes on the porch, then barges backward into the kitchen. He's bent by the weight of a box, turning to set it on the table.

"Go slowly," says Hannah. He's puffing. "Ask Squid to give you a hand."

"I can do it," he says. "Nothing I haven't done a thousand times before."

He puts down the box and he leans his weight on the table.

"At least sit for a minute," she says. "Have a cup of tea."

He shakes his head. "The wee one hasn't eaten."

"There's plenty here," she says, but already Murray's on his way.

There are steaks and pork chops, a roast of lamb. They're wrapped in brown paper stained with blood. She lifts them out and stacks them on her arm. She takes them to the freezer, down a trail that's worn in the white linoleum.

At the bottom of the box she finds a tin that's flat and heavy. Without a thought, just by habit, she takes a chair to push the tin to the back of the highest shelf, behind the oven cleaner and ammonia. Then, leaning across the gap, her hand braced on the cupboard door, it occurs to Hannah that she hasn't done this in years, though once she did it every month. And she climbs down from the chair still holding the tin.

When Murray comes in she's clicking her fingernail against the narrow key soldered to its back.

"This is the end of it," says Murray. With his hip he pushes the door shut. He lets his box slide to the table. "Eggs in here. Mind you don't break them."

"Murray?" she says. "What possessed you to buy oysters?"

He stares at the tin, at the chair, at the cleaning cupboard with its door hanging open. "Oh," he says. "I don't know."

"I started to hide them," she says. "I was thinking— Murray, you haven't bought oysters in years."

They were Squid's favorite food; she could go through a tin in a minute, picking the oysters out with her fingers, slurping the juice until it dribbled down her chin. Every Christmas there was a tin of oysters in her stocking.

Then Murray, in his daily lectures on biology, chose mussels as his subject. They grew on the steep-sided shore to the south, in clusters on the reefs. He tore a big one free and said, "Gather round." He always said "Gather round" to start it off. Squid was six or seven.

Hannah, Squid, and Alastair sat on rocks as sharp as nails. "This is the byssus," said Murray, spreading with his fingers the cottony threads that held the mussel to its rock. "It's spun by a gland in the animal's foot. He lashes himself in place, like Ulysses to his mast."

He turned the shell in his hand. It was a California mussel, nearly eight inches long. He pointed out the scars along the shell, like patches of white on its deep purple back. "This fellow," he said, "has had some sort of an accident. He might have been whacked by a log." The scars were deep, and Murray picked at the grooves with his nails. "The poor brute almost bought it there. Must have got the fright of his life."

"How old is he?" asked Alastair.

"Hard to say." Murray bounced the mussel in his palm. "He's an old-timer, all right. They grow like weeds in the beginning; more than three inches the first year. But then they slow down, and this one's lived on the island maybe as long as I have."

"Wow!" said Squid.

"He's terribly strong," said Murray. "Stronger than any of us. Just try to pull him open." He made everyone have a try. Alastair grunted and frowned. Squid rapped it on the rock, and a chip of shell flew off. Then Murray pulled out his clasp knife and shoved it through the hinge.

"Sorry, old man," he said to the mussel. There was a tearing sound as he pried it open.

"He's screaming!" shouted Alastair.

"No, no," said Murray. "That's only his hinge you're hearing." He held the opened mussel, and the children leaned over him, one on each side. At their feet, the swell surged at the rock.

"Why's he so orange?" said Alastair.

They had all seen the insides of mussels before. But Hannah, too, was always surprised by the lurid color, a ghastly orange bright as boiled yams. She had never thought to wonder why the mussel looked like that.

"It's just the way he is," said Murray. "Colorful, flamboyant." He poked at the flesh with the tip of his knife. "It sets him apart from the oysters and the clams. He's the man-about-town of the shellfish family."

"Is he related to oysters?" asked Alastair.

Murray nodded. "Like brothers."

"But oysters aren't orange," said Alastair.

"No. They're too sedate for that," said Murray. "An oyster wouldn't dare to be orange. He has a shell as thick as armor, but he likes his water deep, where the waves won't knock him about. That's typical for the shellfish to be timid like that. The whole lot of them are utterly harmless, locked up in their shells all their lives. Oysters especially so. They're not nearly as outgoing as a snail."

Alastair poked at the orange goo. "Where's his brain, Dad?"

"He has no brain," said Murray. "No heart or lungs. He breathes water through his gills, and most of him's a stomach. Like the oyster, he's a simple, stay-at-home sort of creature, happy to munch away all day on microscopic plants and animals." He poked harder at the mussel, burying the knifepoint inside it. "No pearl in this one. Not that it would be worth anything if there was. And of course we won't eat him. Tell me why not."

"Red tide!" shouted Squid.

Murray grinned. "Right you are. If our friend here has been eating the wrong sort of things he could be loaded with poisons. So we'll just put him back on the rock."

He set the mussel gently on top of the others.

"Will he lash himself down?" asked Alastair.

"I'm afraid not," said Murray. "He's a goner now, rest his soul." He closed his knife and slipped it into his pocket, twisting his hip up from the stone. He rubbed his hands together. "Well, any questions?"

There never were at question time.

"Then, there being none, we'll break into teams for a wrestling game. Men against the girls."

The memory is vivid to Hannah. She can still hear Squid's happy shout. She can feel the wind in her hair, and the rock under her feet as she stood for the run to the beach. She can smell the sunburned skin above her lip and feel the glare from the sea in her eyes.

But Alastair stayed where he was, hunched and small, beside the clutch of mussels.

"Come on!" said Murray. "You'll let down the team."

Alastair looked up at him, like a worried little gnome. "We shouldn't eat oysters," he said. "It isn't right."

Squid laughed. "It isn't right," she mocked, grinning with the sunlight bright in her hair.

"Shhh!" said Murray. He knelt beside Alastair. "It's the natural process," he said. "The oyster eats plankton; something eats the oyster; something else eats that. This mussel here, he's not a waste. When the tide comes in, some sea star will wander along and think himself very lucky not to have to jack him open."

"But he's harmless," said Alastair. "He lives in his shell and never comes out." He touched the flesh one more time. Already it was drying to a hard, dead thing. "He's all dark and nearly black on the outside. And inside he's so soft and pretty. It isn't right to kill him."

He was describing himself; Hannah can see that now. He was describing just the way he would be in a few more years, a dark and brooding child, so tender inside. And suddenly that day, he burst into tears.

"Why are you crying?" asked Squid.

" 'And all the little Oysters stood and waited in a row'!"

In the kitchen of the big house, Hannah smiles at the memory. Then Murray, seeing her, says, "You look so sad, Hannah."

She sniffs. She wipes her cheeks, and it surprises her to find them wet. "He quoted from 'The Walrus and the Carpenter.' Remember that?"

And Murray laughs. It's not his old laugh, so deep and loud that it almost hurt to hear it. He *chuckles*, as though he doesn't want—or mean—to laugh.

"Poor Alastair," he says. "He never ate another oyster after that."

She wants to tell Murray now that she saw him. That the island has not one ghost, but two. In the single flash of light, as he stood on the lawn staring in, Alastair looked healthy and full-blooded and strong. He wasn't wearing glasses.

She puts the oysters on the counter, but it bothers her to have them there. She tucks the tin sideways behind the rack of dishes, aware that Murray's watching.

"Do you ever think that he's near?" she asks. "Do you ever have a sense that he's close?"

"Not so much anymore," says Murray. He starts to collect the empty boxes, pushing one inside another. "At first I did. I'd be walking down the trail and I'd think he'd come and walk behind me. I heard him laughing once. I thought I saw him get up from a rock—och, a hundred yards away—and hurry off along the sand." The boxes squeak as he pushes them down. "I think there were a couple of times when I went up to his room. Did you know that?"

"No," she says. It was many times more than a couple.

"I always had the feeling he was there. That he'd been there just a moment before. But it's gone now, that sense of that. He's cleared off, I think."

He bends at the knees and picks up the stack of boxes. "Anything else for burning?" he asks.

Hannah shakes her head.

He goes out to the porch and puts on his shoes. He reaches back to close the door. "I made them work too much," he says. "I should have taken more time for play." Then the door clicks shut, and he cocks his head at her through the square of glass. He gathers his boxes and goes thumping down the steps, peering round the cardboard.

He, too, is like the mussel, she thinks. He's rooted to his island; his byssus is just as strong. To tear him loose would kill him.

She watches him head along the path, and thinks it's sad that he has to pass the wailing wall just now, and again, with every load of boxes. Painting that little row of stones was Alastair's first job. He was two years old, and he cried himself along the row, but Murray kept him at it until every stone was painted.

Sure enough, Murray stops there for a moment, and Hannah pities him for that. He's being too hard on himself. There was lots of time for play.

Hannah puts a colander full of cherries in the sink. She turns on the tap, and a moment later, the pump switches on in the basement, humming below her feet. The water flows up from the cistern, pouring over her hands.

It never took more than three hours to do the work around the station. In winter it seldom took one. And then, apart from the weathers—a ten-minute job every three hours—the days were theirs to spend as they would.

They shed their coveralls and painting caps, their gardening gloves and work boots.

"Tools," said Murray. And they went and hung them on their pegs, matching each one to the proper silhouette from the dozens that Murray had drawn on nearly every wall.

They put on bright-colored clothes of red and yellow and pink. Even Murray sometimes dared to wear an ocher-colored shirt. And then they ran; they flew. They pounded down the boardwalk, leaning at the bends, Murray in the lead, then Squid, then Alastair, spinning and leaping—squawking—flying across the island like a flock of parrots. Over the muskeg and into the forest, past the squirrels' middens and the aeries of the eagles, plucking up feathers and ferns and running on, falling—at the end—onto the sand, dropping lemming-like into a laughing, squirming heap.

They lived at the beach, by the sea. Murray unslung Hannah's kayak from the basement rafters, painted it red, and carried it down to the beach. He built a rowboat from the plywood of his packing crates, and set a thick pane of glass into the bottom. And they drifted all around the little lagoon, out through the gap to the channel, down to the point where the ocean swells burst in a rage on the rocks.

Hannah turns off the water. She shakes the cherries, gladdened somehow by their splash of brightness.

Those were the happiest days of her life, in that funny little boat, with the black stenciled message Handle With Care showing through Murray's white paint like a shadow. She loved to stare through the glass as the beach dropped away, as the water got deeper and darker. And then a rock would glide past, or a strand of kelp, and suddenly the bottom would zoom up toward her, gaudy with starfish and anemones.

One day, as they floated at low tide over an always-drowned reef, Murray threw out a stone for an anchor. And they huddled round the pane of glass like Gypsies at a crystal ball. There were urchins below them, like a shelf full of pincushions.

"The urchin," said Murray, beginning a lecture. "Another animal that starts life as a wanderer and settles down when he's older. Some of them sit so long in one place that they wear hollows in the rock."

"They look like porcupines," said Squid, who had never seen a porcupine.

"Indeed they do," said Murray. "The urchin protects himself with a fistful of swords, but it's all for show; he never attacks another creature. If the ground was softer he'd turn his swords to plowshares and dig himself a pit. And if something comes after him, he won't try to poke it. Most likely, he'll run away, racing on his swords."

They saw that too, a few days later. Through the glass of the boat, they saw the urchins hurtling along in an awful slow motion, climbing over one another, dropping from boulders and cliffs. They looked like panicked, stampeding cattle.

"Starfish coming," said Murray. And sure enough, behind them came a big, lumbering sea star, a bogeyman crawling along. "They're actually related. Close as cousins. But there's no love lost there."

The urchins' spines waved and shook. They reached forward; they pushed from behind, and the urchins went tumbling along.

"Poor things," said Alastair. "What will happen if the starfish catches them?"

"He'll eat them, stupid," said Squid. She leaned over the glass. "I'd like to see that. I wish he'd hurry, the stupid star."

Hannah takes a towel from the drawer and lays it out on the counter. She spills the cherries across it, spreading them with her hand. Murray likes to have his cherries blotted dry. Otherwise, he thinks, they'll rot and spoil.

She misses the old days, the lectures. There are things she learned from Murray that she'll always remember, word for word.

"Whelks are cannibals. A hundred babies might grow in their capsule, but only one comes out."

"The hermit crab is a scoundrel, too lazy to build a shell."

The lessons made the children what they were. Alastair was sensitive; Squid was wild. The lessons inspired Hannah to go through Murray's shelf of books, learning all she could of animals she had scarcely looked at before.

Then Alastair turned ten.

And Murray lectured on the barnacle.

~

The cherries spread before her remind Hannah of that day. Crowded on the towel, they're lumps beneath her hand. She touches them softly, gently, the way Alastair touched the barnacles.

"They love company," said Murray, squatting on the rocks below the tower. "They're friendly as all get-out."

Squid was quieter than usual. They'd walked right around the island, and Hannah had feared that Murray wouldn't be giving a lecture that day. But he'd only been watching for a big mass of barnacles, to better illustrate his point. There were so many barnacles she couldn't see the rock underneath them. They covered it like stucco, in clumps as jagged as broken teeth.

"See how they live in cities?" asked Murray. "In high-rises even, one atop another? But as children they go swimming through the ocean. They're as free as butterflies, no shell to weigh them down."

He touched the barnacles. "Gather round," he said.

They found places at his elbows, Alastair right in front of him.

"When a barnacle gets a little older he decides to settle down. He finds a city and gives up his wandering ways; he builds his own little house in the city. And in it he'll live for all his days."

He ran his hand across them. "Look closely," he said.

They all bent down. The wind ruffled round them, and a flock of gulls went by above.

"See how they live? They put up walls, a door at the top. Can you see how the shell is made in plates, with hinges and all the hardware? They've closed up shop because the tide is out, but their doors are still ajar."

Hannah leaned over them. The barnacles dug at her knees and the flesh of her hands. But she saw the doors and wondered how it was that she'd never noticed them before. They were beautifully formed, a pyramid of plates. And they all slammed closed as she brushed her hand across the shells.

Beside her, Alastair was doing it too. She saw his face, the look of magic.

"In every house there's a barnacle," said Murray. "They stick their heads to the rock with cement. The strongest glue in the world. And when the tide comes in they open their doors and poke out their feet. They thrash and kick at anything that drifts by. Their days of swimming are gone forever; they can never leave their houses. And at the slightest danger, they lock themselves inside. They bolt their doors and cower in the darkness."

He stood up. "There," he said. "That's what city life does to you."

Alastair was still staring at the barnacles, still stroking them kindly. Squid sat back and brushed her knees. The skin was red and mottled, speckled with barnacle dust.

"Well," said Murray, his hands on his hips. "Any questions? Then, there being none—"

"Wait!" said Alastair.

Murray frowned. There were never questions at question time.

"How do they . . ." Alastair bit his lip. "You know. How do they—do that?"

"You mean, how do they swim?" asked Murray, hopefully.

"No," said Alastair. "Have babies."

Hannah rolls the cherries under her hand and remembers how the question shocked her. She picks up the towel by its corners, folding them into a bulging ball.

It was inevitable; she can see that now. Not once in his lectures had Murray mentioned reproduction. The lives of his animals began in childhood and ended in lonely solitude.

Of course it was Squid who pressed the point. "Yes, Dad," she said, springing forward again. "How do they do that? How *do* they have babies?"

"Funny you should ask," he said, and scratched furiously at his hair. "I think it was Aristotle who wrote that barnacles grow as seedlings on a tree and drop from there into the water."

Squid giggled. "What a silly guy!"

"Right you are!" Murray laughed. "Well," he said, "I think it's high time—"

But Alastair wasn't about to be put off. He had his fingers spread across the barnacles, a look of worry on his face. "So how do they do it, Dad?"

"It's complicated," said Murray. Flustered, he waved his hands in circles. "You see, barnacles are what are called hermaphrodites." He blushed. He swallowed. He scrunched his face. "It's like a man and a woman living in the same shell; in the same body. So all they have to do is open their doors and let the babies out."

"But that isn't right," said Hannah.

"It most certainly is," he huffed.

"But it's not quite true."

⁓

How many times has she wished she never said that? What did she start on the shore that day? She gets out a bowl and tips the cherries inside it. They tumble from the towel, bouncing into a heap at the bottom. It annoyed her so much that Murray, for the first time, had taught the children a lie.

"They *could* do that," she said. "They *could* have babies themselves. But they usually don't."

There was a strange expression on Alastair's face. She had betrayed his father. And it was a new experience for Hannah when Alastair turned to her instead, and asked her—and not Murray—how the barnacles made their babies.

She didn't look at Murray. She looked at the barnacles.

"They act like couples," she said. "One becomes the man, and its neighbor becomes the woman. The man reaches out with his penis and puts it in the woman's house. She mixes his sperm with her eggs, and sends them out to the sea."

Alastair thought for a moment. "Is that how you and Dad made me and Squid?"

Even Hannah blushed then. "Well, something like that," she said.

Alastair watched her, then nodded briskly as though he understood it all. "Okay," he said. And they broke into teams for a relay race. The men against the girls.

She thought it was over. The children, she imagined, went away with a very puzzling image of Murray locked in the big house and her in the small one, stirring eggs and sperm in a mixing bowl. That was all right; they'd had their talk on the birds and the bees, and it should have been the end of it. But the next day the lesson was scallops, and it was Squid who asked, "How do they make their babies?"

Murray turned at Hannah. He glared accusingly.

Outside, smoke is rising from the burning barrel, torn to wisps by the wind when it reaches the height of the trees. Hannah pushes the bowl to the back of the counter and lays the towel on top. She starts putting eggs in the fridge, dropping them one at a time into the molded cups on the door. She remembers how furious Murray became.

"Look what you've started," he said.

"It's a fad," she told him. "It'll pass."

They sat alone in the living room, the children in bed. There were no curtains on the windows, and outside— across the lawn—the trees flashed white as the beam swung around in the tower.

Murray had a book in his hand. He was picking at the corner of a page. "They're too young for that sort of thing," he said. "When I was twice their age I still thought a stork brought babies in a bundle."

Hannah laughed. "You were twenty years old before you knew where babies came from?"

"Och," he said. "I don't remember."

She tried to picture him at Alastair's age, but all she saw was a smaller Murray. She saw him walking all alone over the scrub and the dust of the badlands, winding past the hoodoos that she could never quite imagine. A boy in khaki shorts, a lonely boy, watching for storks and peering under cabbage leaves.

"What are you smiling at?" he asked. "It's not a laughing matter."

"How did you find out?" she said. "Who told you?"

"The point," said Murray, his teeth together, "the point, Hannah, is that you shouldn't have told them what you did."

"They have to know," she said.

"But not yet. They're not old enough."

"Oh, Murray, they're nearly grown up," she said.

He couldn't see it himself, but they were far beyond their years. They were adults really, in children's bodies, and what wonder was that with only adults for models? Only once had they seen a child, when a technician came in late July to work on the radio beacon and brought his son along for the flight, on a gray and over-cast day.

The boy's name was Todd. He was six, just a year less than Squid. He came out of the helicopter holding his father's hand.

"Look at that!" cried Alastair. "There's a baby on the chopper!"

The technician was tall and thin, big-headed, dressed in green oilskins with a yellow rain hat. He looked like a daffodil as he swayed and nodded toward them, the boy's fist in one hand, an enormous case in the other. He bent himself double to talk to his son. "Daddy has to work," he said. "Why don't you go play with the kids?"

Kids! How she bristled at the sound of that. "Kids are goats," Murray had told her, years before, and she had never used the word again.

"Go play with the kids," the technician said. And Squid looked up at him.

"Actually," she said, "we wanted to watch you work on the transmitter." And Alastair asked, "Have you got an os-cilloscope in there?"

Hannah intervened. "Todd is your guest," she said. "Show him around the station. Maybe he'd like to see the tower."

"Now there's an idea," the technician said. He grinned at his boy. "Would you like to see a lighthouse, Todd?"

"I'll show him how I dangle from the top," said Squid.

Hannah grimaced. "Oh, no you won't."

The three of them went off, poor Todd glancing back. He looked like an explorer being led away by can-

nibals, and she didn't see them for nearly four hours, until the helicopter was due to leave. Then only Alastair
and Todd came out from the forest, covered with burrs,
coated with mud from their feet to their knees, from their
hands to their elbows. Their faces were smeared with
black.

"Where's Squid?" asked Hannah.

"She's coming," said Alastair.

"We went digging in the mizzens," said Todd. "I found
a bit of bone that's a thousand years old!" He held it up, a
tiny shard. "It's part of a skeleton, see?"

Squid came a hundred yards behind them, muttering
to herself, slashing at the grass with a crooked stick. She
didn't realize she'd caught up to the others until she was
right among them. Then she looked up, startled. She flung
the stick away and, crossing her arms, sat down on the
lawn.

It was time for Todd to go. He went with his father,
babbling all the way. "There's mizzens all over the island,"
he said.

"Middens!" shouted Squid. "They're *middens*, you
stupid nut."

Hannah laughs now. She wonders what stories the
technicians took away to tell to their city wives in their
city houses. Did they tell them about children who chat-
tered like adults? About Murray and his strange, rumpled
ways, his set of ideas that he ranted about? "Have you had
any burglaries?" he would always ask. "Any muggings this
morning?" He was obsessed with crime in the city, though
"the city" was only little Prince Rupert, with fewer than

twelve thousand people. And what did they say, those technicians, about Hannah herself? Did they think *she* was odd? She liked long, heavy dresses, and scarves that blew in the wind like the pennants of ships. On a breezy day a sound went with her, a thrumming of cloth, a tramping of Murray-sized boots.

She's standing by the fridge, the door open and all the eggs in their cups, when Murray comes back to the kitchen with his shoes in his hand.

"Tatiana's only three," she tells him.

"What?" asks Murray.

"There's nothing wrong with Tat. We're not used to normal children."

He looks at her blankly, no idea what she's been thinking. Then he shakes his head, stoops, and puts his shoes on the floor. "Och," he says, straightening. "I remember when my brother was three, and he wasn't much like Tat. No Einstein there, but he was far beyond her."

Hannah closes the fridge. A year ago the handle fell off, and Murray crafted another from the crook of a yew. It fits her hand nicely with its curves and its bends. It feels warm in her palm, oiled by her skin.

"Tatiana can't hold a candle to her mother," says Murray. "She's a strange one, and no wonder, with the father what he was."

"You never met him," she says.

"And a good thing for him."

She worries now when Murray's angry. It's not healthy, she thinks, his blood so full of steak and pork. It was a mistake to start along this path. "Yes, you're right," she tells him. "You're quite right, Murray."

"My brother could outshine Tatiana when he was half her age. I remember clearly when he came."

"Oh?" she says. "Was it by cabbage or by stork?"

He looks puzzled. Then the redness in his cheeks brightens.

"Och, you're a funny lady," he says.

chapter six

June 14. Today I turned twelve. No presents from anyone. I nearly cried. Then there was dinner and no cake. We just ate like a normal day, then Mom got up and left, and Squid went after her. And I sat with Dad for a while. Then he said, "Och, I nearly forgot." And he reached in his pocket and took out a key. He said, "This is for you. Happy birthday, son."

He slid it across the table and I picked it up. I thought it was a pretty crummy present, just a key to the house. Then Dad laughed. He said, "Don't look so glum. It's the key to the small house, not this one, you gowk. We're giving you the small house, Alastair."

We went next door and I opened the door. And Squid was there, and Mom, and they were holding a great big cake with all the candles burning. And Squid said, "Look at him! The stupid guy's crying!"

I'm writing in my own house now. MY OWN HOUSE! I can't believe it. Dad says I should name it. He says lots of houses have names. He said, "How about Shangri-La? There's

a nice little name. How about The Wee But and Ben? Or
Glenard. 'The end of the glen,' in the Gaelic."

I said, "Sure. Thanks, Dad."

I'm going to call it Gomorrah!

"Gomorrah?" said Hannah. "Oh no, not that!" She
was shocked, Squid remembers; she stood with her hand
in her mouth staring up at the sign that Alastair made.

"Don't you know," asked Hannah, "what Gomorrah
was?"

"I do," said Alastair. He was disappointed, a little bit
angry. "Gomorrah was the place where the patriarchs went
when they needed more room. The best and the wisest
people went to Gomorrah to live."

Squid laughed. "What an egotist!" she said.

And Alastair whirled on *her.* "You're going to live
here too," he said. He whistled through his nose. "Next
year *you'll* be here. We'll *both* be here when you turn
twelve."

"But not Gomorrah," said Hannah. "It was a wicked
place, Alastair. A wicked, wicked place, and God destroyed it in the end. Oh, Murray, please tell him."

"Och," said Murray. He never got involved in arguments. "Don't you like Shangri-La?" he said.

"No, I don't," said Alastair. He looked like a mouse
cornered by cats. His big glasses shone in the sun. "I'm going to call it *Gomorrah!*"

"I love it when he says that," said Squid.

Hannah flapped her hands. "Murray!" she said.

"Och," he said again. "What's the harm in letting the

boy call the house what he wants? Surely you don't expect God to come down in a fury over a thing like a name."

"Well, thank goodness my father can't see it. He would turn in his grave."

Squid was fascinated. No one had ever argued about anything remotely religious. She had been brought up with only one lesson—to believe in whatever she thought was right.

"I wash my hands of it," said Murray. He walked away—backward. "The name means something to Alastair and something else to you. But to me it means nothing at all. I can't imagine that one city is any more wicked than another."

He turned then, and started to run. Hannah glared after him. She said, "Alastair, I can't tell you what to call the house. But will you please think about what I said?"

"Okay. You want to come in?"

"I don't think so," she said. "I'm sorry, but not today."

Only Squid was left to go inside. And she remembers now, with the diary in her hands, how Alastair had made the house all ready for his visitors. There were four glasses on the coffee table, a jug of purple juice dripping water on its outside. He'd cut up carrots and arranged them in an awful, fussy way, with wedges of tomato and sticks of celery and cheese. He'd made chains out of paper, and hung them from the corners of the room, and he went to the middle and self-consciously pulled on a string.

Confetti fell down, a shower of papery bits. They dropped in a lump onto his head and his shoulders, and trickled down to a heap at his feet.

"Welcome to Gomorrah," he said.

June 16. *The big housewarming was a washout.*

June 17. *I'm going to build a room in the attic. You'll get there up a spiral staircase right through the living room, up two floors to big skylights. If you stand at the bottom it will look like you're climbing up to the sky. I'll put in glass walls and gather some birds that can fly around at the top. I think I can catch them under cardboard boxes baited with oatmeal. And that way I can pick out the ones I want and the others won't get hurt. No birds will be harmed! I swear to that.*

She never knew what he'd done with the boxes. She found him burning them, ripping them into shreds, ramming the pieces down in the barrel. The flames gouted up, orange and swirling, and he cringed from the heat as he worked. Ashes soared round and around, billowing up as high as the tower, leaping from the barrel in crinkles of red, turning to gray and to black as they rose.

"What are you doing?" she asked.

"What does it look like?" he said. "I'm burning this stuff. This junk."

It was too hot to stay anywhere close. She wandered away. And down at the edge of the forest, where the alders she'd cut in the spring were already the height of her knees, she found the feathers and the corpses. She knew minks had got the birds; minks always chewed off the heads. And the poor birds lay huddled, headless, half-covered with their wings. There were four of them, in nearly a line, their bodies clotted with blood.

June 18. A *disaster. God forgive me for what I've done.*

June 19. *Started work on the spiral staircase. I'll put paper birds at the top. I can make them out of origami, shiny birds, and the convection currents will make them fly. Dad could do this job in a couple of days. It looks like I'll be done in a week.*

He was back at the burning barrel, feeding it bits of splintered wood, pieces of old packing crates. "Oh, hi," he said as she stepped through the little white gate in the fence that Murray had made.

He tossed another piece of wood into the fire. It was cracked down the middle, bristling with twisted nails.

"I'm useless," he said. "Do you know that?" There was ash on his glasses, and he pulled his sleeve down over his fingers to wipe at the spots on the lenses. "I can't even drive in a nail. I can't even make a dumb staircase."

"Why would you want to?" she asked.

He shrugged. "I can *see* it. I know what I *want* it to be. But when I start to do the work it all falls apart. I wanted a loft up there, a turret like a castle. I tore everything down and made shelves instead." He laughed. "They're junk."

"Ask Dad to help you."

"No," he said. "Dad can't go in there. I don't want him to see what a *crummy* job I'm doing. What would he say?"

"He'd say, 'Let me help you.' "

"No. He'd say, 'Och, let me *do* it.' But Gomorrah's *my* house, Squid. It's mine. And if he gets started he'll make it into something else."

They went to the small house, and Alastair giggled as he showed her the shelves. They tilted and sagged; there were gaps, and the paint wasn't right. He'd put a rope around them to hold the bottom in place. "I'd tear them out," he said. "But I cracked the plaster. There's a gouge in the wall as big as my fist."

Upstairs, he'd cut this hole where she's sitting now, where he hid the diaries long ago.

"I thought I'd start at the top and go down," he said. "And then I realized: I don't have a clue what I'm doing."

"You can't be good at everything," she said.

But he was. He was a genius at most things. And when he saw he couldn't hammer a nail, he just stopped; and he never hammered another one. It was the same with water-color painting. When his first picture wasn't perfect, he gave it up. Alastair was good at everything because he only did the things that he was good at.

Squid puts the book down and takes up another. Suddenly she's in the spring of his fourteenth year, and he has less than seven months to live. She can see him, gangly and pale, going hunched through the rain, in a darkness of noon, in their world of gray.

April 22. *A southeaster. A snorter, Dad would call it. For three days now there's been nothing but wind and rain. I'm so sick of this place. I feel like I've come from a shipwreck, and I'm just waiting here for someone to come and rescue me. The natives are getting restless and I . . .*

Squid laughs. It was a phrase that Alastair picked up from a radio program, a slogan they used often. Murray would get mad over a job poorly done, or Hannah would shout at a door left open, and they would look at each other—Alastair and Squid—and, grinning, say, "The natives are getting restless."

. . . and I keep remembering the Odd Fellow.

She stares at the name. She touches it on the page, imagining that her fingers can sense the thickness of the ink.

It was Alastair who saw the *Odd Fellow*'s flare.

For him, with the rain on his glasses, it was nothing more than a spot of red, a blur, and he came racing into Gomorrah to get her. The wind shrieked through the door as he tore it open. "A flare!" he shouted.

She went outside; he dragged her out. She saw the black shapes of flailing trees; she saw a wooden seagull, a whirligig bird, lift from its perch and cartwheel past the flower bed. She heard the bell ring on the porch of the big house as its clapper swung in the wind. Alastair held her shoulders and aimed her toward the sea. And a moment later, through the sideways-falling rain, she watched a line of red fizzle through the storm.

They ran together, down the path and up the steps of the big house. Murray and Hannah were in the kitchen, sitting close together on separate chairs. They huddled up to the radio as they would to a fireplace, leaning forward, their heads turned away from the speaker. They looked up as Squid and Alastair burst into the room.

"You *know?*" said Alastair. "You know all about it?"

"Shhh!" Murray held up a hand. He reached forward and turned up the volume.

"Mayday, mayday!" The voice was a man's. It was

screaming. "Oh, Christ, aren't you coming? Jesus God, I'm going down."

"How long have you known?" said Alastair. "How long have you sat here and listened?"

No one answered. On the *Odd Fellow*, the man was crying. "The windows are busted. The waves are coming straight in. My arm's . . . She's going over. She's going *over*! Oh, God, can't you help me?"

Alastair stared at the speaker. His face was like whitewash.

"I'm dead! I'm dead!"

"Do something!" said Alastair. "Oh, Dad, please can't you do something?"

Again, Murray reached out. He turned the dial, and the radio clicked and went off. "That's all I can do," he said. The wind wailed past the roof and banged at the window; the rain gurgled and howled in the pipes. Outside, the surf was like a deep and steady drumming. The bell rang again on the porch, but the kitchen seemed silent.

"We don't have to listen," said Murray. "I'm sorry; that's the best I can do."

Alastair flung himself out through the door. He ran into the blackness, into the storm. Squid went after him. Murray and Hannah came after him too, their chairs falling back on the floor.

He ran over the grass, through a whirlwind of spray, out to the bridge where the waves reared up and crashed through the gap in a thunder of sound.

"No!" shouted Hannah, but he headed across it. He vanished into a wall of white-tipped water. The sea came over the bridge. It leapt up the rail, surging round the posts, squirting through the gaps in the planks. The beacon turned, and the wave was huge in the flash of hot white light. Then it fell away, booming down on the rocks. And there was Alastair, climbing up the slope on the far side, staggering to the edge of the island, toward the flare he'd seen.

Murray started to follow, but Hannah clung to him. "No," she said. "Murray, no!" And Squid went instead. They shouted her name; Murray bellowed at her to stop. But she kept going, over the path and onto the trestle, her head down as she ran. A wave rose in foam that covered her shoulders, and she groped for the rail as the water tugged her feet across the planks toward the edge. Her head went under; she held her breath, then gasped and carried on.

Alastair stood on the very last bit of land. He had his fists in the air, shaking them, shaking his arms and his hair and his thin, narrow chest. Squid held on to him, and the wind tore at them both. The surf raged up at their feet.

"Damn you, God!" he shouted. "Damn you, damn you, damn you."

The helicopter arrived at daybreak, as the storm was finally easing. It fluttered back and forth across the sea. Back and forth, back and forth. And then wreckage came ashore: bits of wood; a red running light in a broken frame; a quilted comforter that oozed like a huge blue jellyfish onto the sand. Up came the dead man's boots, the dead man's coat, the dead man's plastic thermos. Everything that washed ashore, Murray nudged at with sticks until it drifted off again.

But Alastair stayed in bed. For three days he never moved.

"He just lies there and cries," said Squid. No one was allowed through the door. "I don't think he's crying for the dead man so much as for himself."

"He's not ashamed, is he?" asked Hannah.

Squid shook her head. "It isn't that, Mom. He says he's crying because he found out that there isn't a God."

On the fourth day, he came out from his room. He went quietly to the window and curled up on the seat. In the sunlight he looked as pale and soft as an oyster out of its shell.

"I cracked," he said. "Didn't I?"

"Alastair, it's all right," she said.

"No. I snapped. I did." He gazed over the lawn. Murray had carted off the kelp and the tangles of sticks two days before, and there was nothing to show that a storm had gone by. "I don't know if I can take it," he said. "One day I'll just go crazy. I'm sure of it, Squid. I'll go nuts."

Squid sits on the floor and stares at the words that Alastair wrote.

chapter seven

"COULD YOU GO FIND SQUID?" ASKS HANNAH. "She's at the small house, I think."

"At the small house?" says Murray. "On delivery day?"

It would have been unthinkable once. She and Alastair, as children, would hover in the kitchen as Murray brought the boxes in. They would marvel at the cherries as though they'd never seen such a thing. They would sit backward on the chairs or perch on the table or the countertop, peering in the boxes, shouting out, "Bananas!" Or, "Crumpets!" Murray always ordered crumpets. Or, "Oh, yuck, asparagus!"

"We should have waited," says Murray. "Tatiana's just the age to appreciate delivery day." He's holding his shoes again, fingers curled in the heels. "We'll make a McCrae of her yet."

"She's already a McCrae," says Hannah.

"Not really." He closes the door as he speaks, to let himself have the last word. "She's only half a McCrae, I'm afraid."

Hannah stares at the door, through its window at Murray retreating. She wants to ask: What about me? What about Alastair and Squid? Aren't we *all* only half McCraes? But she knows what he means. Tatiana's father was an Outsider.

～

His name was Erik. "Erik with a *k*," said Squid at the time. He came to the island by kayak, all alone, just as Hannah had come years and years before. He camped on the beach where she had camped. He, too, was startled by the auklets.

But Hannah didn't see him, and Murray didn't see him.

"He had a beard and long hair," said Squid. "He looked like a Viking." He paddled a boat that rose up at the bow, in a curve like the neck of a swan. He made a fire in a scraped-out pit in the sand, and he lay on his back, reading poems by Keats. This is what Squid told them had happened.

"He read me a poem," she said. "It was beautiful, like it was just for me. He read me a poem, and he told me how pretty I was."

He had a tent with flags on the poles. He read her a poem and then . . .

Hannah doesn't want to think of this. She busies herself with the big sacks of lentils and rice, tearing them open, setting out the storage jars. But she can't stop herself from seeing the things she's seen a hundred times. Squid, a child, taking off her clothes, laying them in the sand. Erik watching in the firelight, helping with the buttons.

"No!" says Hannah, aloud. The rice swirls out of the bag and into the jar, mounding against the glass.

Squid was so young. A beautiful girl—yes, maybe a woman—but only thirteen. She made jewelry out of pretty shells. She liked to go barefoot at the edge of the water. She liked to weave daisies into chains.

It was Murray's fault, what happened. Hannah might have started it, but Murray never stopped it. She had warned him that something awful lay waiting. She had known it ever since Alastair was ten, and the giggling sounds had come out of the forest.

She was on the south side of the island, where the trees went right to the rocks, and the rocks right to the water. She heard Squid and Alastair playing among the hemlock trees. She had to climb over lichen-spotted boulders to see what they were up to.

Otters lived there. They dug dens out of the earth at the roots of the trees. Some of the holes were enormous.

Hannah used branches to pull herself up. She stepped from the rocks to the dirt. And she stopped when she saw what the children were doing.

They were upside down. Alastair had his head in an otter den; Squid had hers in another. They were holding themselves on their elbows less than a yard apart. Squid's dress had fallen around her, and her stomach was bare—and her chest—so smooth and pale. Her legs kicked from white panties, her red shoes flailing. Alastair's feet groped like tentacles, like stalks of blue in his overalls.

Suddenly, from the ground, burst another chorus of muffled giggles. Then Alastair's foot touched Squid's, and she trapped it between her ankles.

Hannah rushed forward. She pried the children apart, pulling on Alastair's foot, pushing on Squid's. She knocked them down, and their heads popped out of the dens. Their faces were flushed; they stared up at her. Alastair had caught his ear on a bit of root, and he rubbed it with his hand.

She said, "What are you doing? What on earth are you doing?"

"Nothing," said Squid, in her cheery voice, chirpy as a songbird. "We were playing barnacles."

"Well, stop it," said Hannah. "Squid, pull your dress down. Just look at you both!" There were twigs in their hair, old and blackened leaves wedged in their collars and cuffs.

Alastair kept rubbing his ear. "We were only playing," he said.

Squid grinned. "He was trying to put his penis in my house."

"Stand up," Hannah told them. "Both of you."

They got up. They stood there, adjusting their clothes, and something in Hannah's voice or her look must have scared them.

"We were only playing," said Alastair again.

"Then you just play on the beach," she said. "And not another word from either of you."

⌒

Hannah tilts the bag to stop the flow of rice. A few grains skitter over the top of the jar, and she collects them with her fingers and pops them into her mouth. She moves down the table and starts on a second jar.

She never told Murray what the children had been doing at the otter dens. But a week later she woke at midnight in a bed that seemed empty without Murray. And thinking about it, she couldn't fall asleep again. She put a coat over her nightgown, rubber thongs on her feet, and stepped out through the door, down the steps into an ocean of stars.

The sea was utterly calm. There was no wind and no swell, and the water lapped at the shore as soft as cat tongues. The Milky Way was a shimmering bracelet of diamonds that girdled the sky and looped right around through the sea. Every star was mirrored on the water. And the beacon turned round and round, a huge propeller of light with blades that paled against them.

Her thongs slapped on the concrete. It must have been the dew; it was all she could guess. But something had brought the frogs up to the lawn, onto the path. And they crouched down as she passed, or went crawling away in slow-stretching bounds, as though the moisture held them like glue.

She crossed the bridge and climbed the slope, and found Murray sitting at the base of the tower. He was staring off to the southeast, toward Triple Island far away, a faint and tiny version of the beacon right above them.

"Fog's coming," he said, hearing her thongs. "Green Island's obscured already."

She nestled beside him, arranging the coat across her knees. Murray seemed so peaceful and calm, so contented, that she shivered as she planned what to say.

Everything comes to an end, she would tell him. She would give him one more year on Lizzie Island, and then they would move to the city. It is time that the children go to a real school, she would say. They should have friends their own age. It's not right, she would say, to raise them in isolation, with no idea of a world outside. She was going to say, "In captivity."

She coughed; she started to speak. But Murray reached out and put a hand on her knee. He said, "Hannah, I think we're about the luckiest people in the world."

"Oh?" she said.

"Why, sure we are." His fingers squeezed, and he smiled. "Och, we've no money in the bank. We're dirt poor if you think about it. But we've got all this." He lifted his hand and made a small, shy gesture. "We've got two healthy children and a paradise to live in, free of crowds and smoke and noise."

It wasn't exactly true. There had been one day, several years before, when electricians came to rewire the light. To do it, they had to shut down the generators. Hannah was outside when they pulled the switch. It was sunny and calm, a wonderful day. Then suddenly there was silence. There was total, absolute silence. For the very first time she heard *nothing*. No machines or generators, no fans or radio noise. And it was eerie, even scary. She was actually frightened at first.

But at the same time, what Murray had said was true. He'd listed the things she liked best about Lizzie.

He put his hand back on her knee. He rubbed it, as he might rub at the head of a dog. "And what does it matter," he said, "what goes on in Russia or Cuba or Korea or anywhere else? What scrap of difference does it make whether you know or don't know which group of people is killing which other group of people?" He glanced toward her. "It matters not a whit."

She said, "No man is an island."

Instantly, the mood changed. Murray stopped talking, and she felt the silence; it closed round them like a fog. A fish, or maybe a seal, splashed below the tower. Murray turned his head and looked off toward Barren Island, its prick of light flashing far away, a fallen star among the thousands.

She nudged him with her elbow. "What's wrong?" she asked.

He said, "You don't agree with me."

"Oh, but I do," she said. "I love it here."

"But this is the end," he said. "Or the beginning of the end. Children start growing, a mother starts talking of schools and friendships. And the next thing you know, another lightkeeper moves to town. It's always the wives. One day they start thinking, and the next they start packing."

"Oh, come on," she said. But he was pretty close to the target.

He said, "I've seen it happen twenty times or more."

She couldn't deny it was what she'd been thinking. But neither would she admit it.

"Well, I'll grant you this," said Murray. "You've outlasted most of them, Hannah. Most of them are gone in two or three years."

"I love you, Murray," she told him.

"Well, it won't happen here." His accent was thicker, stronger. "I'll not be moved from here, Hannah. Not by hell or high water. I watched my father go coughing into the coal mines for eight years. I saw a toilet bowl full of black spittle. And when they buried him, when they threw down the first bits of earth, the sound they made—I thought it was him coughing."

"Murray," she said.

"My brother's still in the mines. He always will be. He was trapped by a cave-in when he was just seventeen."

Finally he stopped. He must have thought that if he said one more word, she would know that he was crying.

She wanted to hold him, but knew he wouldn't let her. She said, "I wouldn't ask you to do that."

And then he did cry. "There's nothing bloody else I can do!" he said, and jumped to his feet.

She said, "Murray. Don't leave me like this."

"Och, I'm not leaving you," he said. "The fog's coming in."

She could still see Triple Island. Even the little light at Barren. But when she looked up, the Milky Way was shrouded in a feathery veil. The beacon whirled ghostly arms. She got up too; she couldn't sit there with the foghorn going.

The tower door was open, spilling yellow light across the blackness. Murray was bent over the motor, turning the crank. It started, and gray smoke spat from the exhaust hole beside her. The compressor rattled, building pressure.

Murray studied his gauges. "All right, Hannah," he said. "You might as well go."

She didn't know right then if he meant for her to go from the tower, or go from the island. She set off back to the trestle, her thongs whapping against her soles. And just as she crossed the gap, she heard the first blast of the horn, a deep and mournful bellow of sound that she felt as well as heard. It rattled in her jaw and rattled in her head; it shook inside her ears. Three seconds later she heard it a second time, and again after three seconds more. There'd be forty-eight seconds of silence, and another three blasts. And so it would go, hour after hour, until someone shut off the motor.

At the house, the front window rattled with the sound. In the kitchen, the dishes quivered in their rack; the spoons and forks shivered in their nests. Hannah went up the stairs.

The children were asleep in their bunks, Alastair above and Squid below. Before winter had come, Murray would put up a wall and carve the room in two, giving them each a tiny space. He would do it at her insistence. But that night, as they always had, they slept in their bunks. And when the horn blew, their eyelids twitched; but they didn't come awake. Only on the first foggy night of the summer would the horn keep them from sleeping.

<hr>

Hannah tops off the second jar and puts down the bag. It's half-empty, swollen at the bottom, flaccid at the top. She reels the jar around on its rim, settling the rice with a rumbling sound.

Murray never came back to bed that night, and not because of the fog. Falling at night, in the middle of summer, it would still be there at noon. She heard his footsteps on the path and, looking out, watched him pass toward the boardwalk. Then she lay awake till dawn, wondering if Murray was right, if it really was the beginning of the end. She thought she'd set them all rushing to a downfall, as though she'd pushed them into the currents of a quickening river.

There wasn't another word spoken about sex until Squid, nearly thirteen, came to the kitchen of the big house. She was crying, and that was unusual for Squid. "There's something wrong with me," she said. "I think I'm busted up inside."

Squid hauled up her skirt. Her white underpants were clotted with red. She held up the skirt for only a moment, then dropped it again. "Oh, Mom," she said. "Am I dying?"

"No, Squid," said Hannah. "Oh, sweetheart." She took her daughter into the bathroom. She locked them up, and Squid sat on the furry cover of the toilet seat to learn what Hannah called, uncomfortably, "the ways of the world."

The talk, as short as it was, left Hannah exhausted.

chapter eight

December 1. *I'd hate for anyone to know this, but I'm lonely by myself. Sometimes I hear them laughing in the big house and I wish I could be there. I see the lights on in all the windows and it makes Gomorrah seem dark and lonely. It's so empty that I talk to myself. I keep hoping that Dad will come over, but he never does.*

What if he gave me Gomorrah to get me out of the way? Maybe they all voted on it. Maybe they said, "We have to get rid of Alastair. It would be so much nicer without Alastair here."

Winter's so long. It's cold and gray and dreary, and it just goes on and on forever. Christmas will come and what if they don't ask me over? I'd hate to spend Christmas alone.

I can hardly wait for Squid's birthday. It will be okay when Squid's over here. But what if she decides not to come?

She looks up at the sound of someone walking on the path. She feels her heart give a sudden, hard beat as the footsteps rise to the porch. Four books lie open around her; she has been moving forward and backward through Alastair's life. She gathers them quickly, slamming them closed and stuffing them in the hole. She slides the floorboards into place. But they don't quite fit. They meet in the middle, making a tent down their length. Then someone knocks on the door.

It's Murray, she knows, his old knock echoing through time, that little rap-a-tap-tap. She presses at the boards, but still they won't move. Murray knocks again.

She rips out the boards and slides one over top of the other. Alastair's old, bent nails rasp on the floor. They leave silver scratches in the varnish. She looks for Tatiana, and is surprised to see that her daughter isn't there.

The door opens downstairs. A draft of air rushes past her. The boards thunk into place and she drags the rug over top; it doesn't quite match the faded oval that it covered so neatly before.

"Squid?" He calls to her. He comes into the living room, directly below. "Squid, are you here?"

He knows where she is; she's sure he knows. Already, he's walking toward the stairs.

"I'm coming down," she says.

He's waiting at the bottom, just as he was the last time, staring up toward her. Squid feels a prickle at her neck, a tensing of her muscles. She'll tell him she has a right to do what she wants, that the house was hers as much as his, that she was Alastair's only friend.

"Look," says Murray, and she gathers her breath.

"Shhh," he says. He reaches up the banister, his fingers in the air. He smiles and shows her with a nod—with a gesture—that Tatiana is sleeping in the armchair, on her back across the cushion with her legs jutting stiffly up the back.

"Out like a light," he says, with a tenderness she's forgotten. He takes her hand, and she remembers that; his fingers are thick and hard and cold. "You used to sleep like that," he tells her. "Like a dog, like a puppy, however you flung yourself down. She must have learned it from you."

"She's never seen me sleep like that," says Squid.

"Och, I meant it well." He turns around; his smile is gone. "Your mother's made a little supper. When you've got the Tatty ready, you can come and eat."

"I think I'll leave her, Dad," she says. "It's better that she sleeps."

"She has to eat," says Murray.

"I'll bring her something."

"I think—" He stops. "Och, I suppose you know best. I've done my duty; I've passed on the message."

⌒

They go together down the path, past the whirligigs and flower beds. Just beyond Gomorrah there's a horse with wings. It's painted red and white.

"That one was your favorite," says Murray. "Remember what you used to call him?"

"Yes," says Squid.

"Old Glory. You used to lie here on the grass and watch him flap his wings. You pretended that you rode him."

They've stopped below the horse. It surprises her now, with its outlandish colors, its odd-shaped head that looks more like a pig's than a horse's.

"You said you were the only one who could ride him. Even I couldn't do that. Old Glory would throw me off, you said."

"I remember, Dad," she says.

"Do you remember that you used to feed him?"

"No," she says.

"You'd pluck some grass and hold it up. You'd say, 'Come on, Old Glory, here's a bit of hay.' " Murray laughs. "You were so serious about it."

"Oh, yeah," says Squid. It's funny she'd forgotten. She can see herself now, standing by the pole, reaching up along it with the grass stems in her fist.

She was absolutely sure the horse could come down if it wanted. "Come on, Old Glory," she'd said. "Just come down and eat."

And didn't it do it once? Didn't it flutter from the pole and pluck the grass away? She can remember the touch of its wooden mouth, the way the lips curled back to show big, yellow teeth that she'd never seen before.

"It made you furious that he never came to eat."

She wants to say, "But once he did." And that was why—because once he did and then not ever again—that she got so mad at Glory.

Squid leans toward the horse. She can barely see the joint that holds one wing together.

"You bashed him with a stick," says Murray. "I said, 'What do you think you're doing?' You said, 'I winged him. He wouldn't eat, so I winged the stupid thing.' "

"You hit me for that," she says. She can still feel the slap, the fingers—so cold and hard—digging into her arm. She dropped the stick and ran away. She hid behind

Gomorrah, though it wasn't called Gomorrah yet, and hauled up the sleeve of her shirt. There were big red marks on her arm, a handprint on her ribs.

"No," says Murray. "I wouldn't do that."

"Yes, you did."

"Och, I never, ever hit you." He looks at her sadly. "I made mistakes, but I never raised a hand to either of you."

"Dad! You did," she says. "You hit Alastair for looking too close at his books."

He doesn't deny it; he just keeps looking at her. "Is this why you've come home, Elizabeth?" he asks. "To dwell on the past and make it worse than it was?"

"Dad!"

"Do you know how many times my father hit *me?*"

"Who cares?" she says. "Alastair was going blind, and you hit him."

"Och, he wasn't going blind. And I certainly didn't hit him."

Murray shakes his head. He shakes it quickly, sighing as he does it. Then he scratches his hair and goes on his way. And Squid follows behind him.

⁓

She was there; she saw it happen. She heard the smack of her father's palm against Alastair's head. It pushed his nose down in the book, and knocked the book from his hand. Then Alastair, without a word, reached down and picked up the book again.

"Hold it away!" said Murray. "Don't bury yourself in the pages."

"It's the only way I can see," said Alastair.

"Then turn on a light. Do you want to go blind?"

"The light doesn't help," said Alastair. He was blinking, staring down at the pages. "The writing's all blurry."

"No wonder," said Murray. "Hold it away, boy. Hold it down on your lap." He thrust out his thick, coppery arm and pushed the book down on Alastair's knee. "There. Read it now."

Alastair swallowed. As the book went down his head went up, pale and frightened. "I can't," he said.

"Try!"

"Dad, it hurts my eyes," said Alastair.

Murray knew the truth then; there was resignation in his eyes. Again, he reached out. He closed the book. He took it up and put it on the table, and his thumb riffled the edge of the pages. Then he held on to Alastair, his arm around the boy's thin shoulders, and he pulled his son against him.

"It will be all right," he said. "Everything will be just fine."

A week later they were on the helicopter, Alastair and Squid and Hannah. They rose from the island and flew to the east, over Melville Island and Chatham Sound, out past the edge of the only world that Squid had ever seen. They flew across Digby Island and over the harbor, and the city spread out below them.

It was smaller than Squid had imagined. She had hoped there would be skyscrapers and great deep canyons they would fly through, past people staring from the windows. Lights of all colors. Masses of cars. Long, silver trains crawling on elevated tracks, stretching round the corners like strings of linked sausage. She had hoped to find a clamor of sirens and bells and horns.

"It's boring," she said, disdainfully. "It's just a boring little city."

But the houses amazed her. They were clumped together, side by side and back to front, house after house after house, like barnacles on a rock, except they stood in tidy rows.

"How can people live like that?" she asked.

They rode in a taxi. The meter impressed her. And the speed! Never in her life had she gone faster over the ground than Murray's little tractor could take her. They sat in the back, three in a row, and she could hear the telephone poles go whumping past the window. And the tires hummed, but that was all the sound there was.

And the city smelled of rotten eggs. But no one seemed to notice.

"It's the pulp mill," said Alastair. "I guess you get used to it."

He came away with glasses that made his eyes look huge. Hannah warned her: "Don't laugh when you see him." And she didn't even want to laugh; she felt like crying.

"I look like a goof," he said. "Don't I?"

"They make you look smart," she said.

"A smart goof." He laughed. "But look, Squid. I can see." He held his hand two inches from his nose, his palm toward his face. "I can see my fingerprints. They look so neat. I've never seen my fingerprints before."

They were thick and clunky glasses. They were wider

than his head, and she could stand behind him and see them jutting out beyond his ears. And sometimes—from behind him—she could see his eyes reflected in the lenses.

"Can you see behind you?" she asked.

"Oh, yes!" he said, and showed her. "See? If I turn my head I can."

They were only gone a week; they couldn't wait to get back, and so they went on the chopper. Alastair on one side, Squid on the other, they watched like explorers for the first sight of their land. Alastair won.

"There it is!" he shouted. "Hello, Lizzie Island." He turned around, and his grin was almost as wide as his glasses. "It looks so beautiful," he said.

chapter
nine

*H*ANNAH CARRIES A PLATTER OUT TO THE
porch, a selection of all the fresh foods, a pile of cherries in
the middle. She puts it down on the table, an old cable
spool that Murray dragged from the beach years ago. She
looks up and sees him coming, with Squid several paces
behind. She's surprised not to see Tatiana.

Murray climbs up the steps and goes right past her,
into the house. He whispers as he passes: "For heaven's
sakes don't ask where the wee one is."

Hannah frowns. What happened in the little house?
she wonders. But Squid isn't any help. She waits till her
father has gone inside, then sits on the steps, facing the
evening sun.

"Hungry?" asks Hannah, touching the platter.

Squid shakes her head.

"But you haven't eaten. And Tatiana—"

"She's sleeping." Squid straightens her legs and lies
back on her elbows, fitting herself to the steps. Her finger-
nails are bright red, her stomach—where it shows below

her blouse—as smooth and white as ivory. "Why's Dad so angry?" she asks.

"He's not."

"Could have fooled me."

Hannah closes her eyes. She doesn't want to be put in the middle of whatever's going on between Murray and their daughter.

"I'm trying to be nice," says Squid. "I'm doing the best that I can." She sighs mightily. "Nothing's ever good enough for Dad," she says.

The door creaks as Murray pushes it open. He's put on his slippers, fuzzy plaids of red and black. They're four years old, but he's still self-conscious when he wears them, thinking their colors too loud and garish. If he heard what Squid was saying, he doesn't let on. He just stands in the doorway, rocking on his feet.

There's a bell hanging there, a big bronze bell with a beautiful knotted lanyard dangling from the clapper. Once that bell hung on the bow of a ship, but it's been on Lizzie so long that even Murray doesn't know the story behind it. He reaches out and runs his fingers over the weaving on the lanyard.

"Come sit with us," says Hannah.

He closes his fist round the lanyard, as though he has to hold on to something.

"Please." Hannah offers again her platter of food, hoping Murray will close the distance between himself and Squid. But no sooner does he shuffle toward them—with a sigh and an "Och" and "I've only got a moment"—than Squid gets up, and stretches.

"I'm sort of wrung out," she says, and starts down the

steps in a slow and languorous way. "I think I'll call it a night."

It's not yet eight o'clock. No one has touched the wonderful food. "I was going to make supper," says Hannah. "One of your favorites, Squid."

"Mom, I said—"

"Canned salmon on toast. Sockeye."

"Whoosh!" Squid presses her hand to her stomach. "I'd never sleep with that." She takes another slow-swinging step. "I guess I'll see you in the morning."

Murray's staring after her. Then he hangs his head and stares at his slippers.

"We love you, Squid," says Hannah.

It felt just this way after that night at the foghorn, when Murray cried to see his world collapsing. They passed through the rooms and the doorways like guests in a grand hotel. They had short, polite conversations.

As far as Squid was concerned, nothing had changed. She went out to her tire swing behind the house and shouted for someone to push her. But Alastair was the sensitive one, and he knew that something was wrong. He asked Hannah: "Are you and Dad having a fight?"

"No," she said. "We had an argument. A discussion."

"About leaving the island?"

"That was part of it, yes." She had no idea how he knew.

"I don't think we should go," he said.

"Why not?"

"Because we'd be so sad if we left."

Once a month the *Darby* came. Or the *Alex Mac*, or the *Bartlet*. They brought the groceries and the diesel fuel. They came loaded with Murray's books, bringing boxes of books as they never had before. There were books on herbs and kangaroos and dinosaurs, on ancient Greece and superstitions. There were travel books from around the world, and even one on photography, though no one owned a camera. Only one thing was missing: any mention of sex.

It seemed to Hannah that Murray had dwelt—in his dogged way—on the business of school and development, and this was his compromise. If correspondence school wasn't enough for the children, they could learn anything else by reading a book.

"Gateways to learning," said Murray, pompously, she thought. As he took each book from the box, he set it onto one of the four stacks he was making: one for each McCrae. Hannah looked at the titles and saw how he was building Alastair and Squid, and even herself, into the people he thought they should be. Alastair would learn how things worked; he would be a great thinker, a philosopher of nature. Squid would be a tinkerer, able to change the things she didn't like, to adapt the world to herself. Hannah looked through her own little pile and saw herself as frivolous, with a narrow range of interests. Murray would know a little bit about everything.

"Here's a good one," he said. "*The Swiss Family Robinson.* It's about people like us."

He held it in his hand, waving it over the table like a sorcerer, trying to decide which pile to put it on. To her surprise, it went to Hannah's.

They read it aloud in the evenings, and all of them were horrified, but none so much as Murray. He must have hoped that it would hold a message for Hannah, how a family—shipwrecked on a strange shore—could build a paradise from nothing.

But the Robinsons spent their days slaughtering every-thing they saw. "They're killing the whales now!" cried Squid. "How can they do that?"

Murray put the book away. He tucked it on a shelf among his tomes on ancient art. But Hannah took it down again and plugged right through to the end. She was disap-pointed; the Robinsons turned out to be sane and normal.

⌒

"What are you thinking?" asks Murray now. He's star-ing down the path toward the small house.

"Oh, I don't know. Just remembering things."

"Bad things or good things?"

She smiles up at him. "There haven't been many bad things," she says.

"I dread the morning," he tells her. "It's like waiting for a storm."

But the new day brings a cheerfulness, a sense of friendship like a relic from the older, happier days of long ago. Squid shows up soon after seven, and Tatiana—barely awake, looking absurdly young in pigtailed hair, dressed again in red from head to toe—almost glues herself to Murray.

Squid wants breakfast on the beach.

"Over a fire," she says. "Eggs and bacon and potatoes. The way we used to do it all the time."

Her memory has fooled her. They only had breakfast on the beach when Murray declared a holiday, and he seldom did that. But it's risking this new mood to point that out.

"Sure," says Hannah. "It's been a long time."

Murray is delighted. "You sit here," he says. "I'll get everything ready."

He brings out buckets and boxes, then loads them onto the tractor, lashing them down with a web of bungee cords stretched in every direction. The kettle at the top sloshes water from its spout.

Squid keeps Tatiana with her, sitting at the edge of the steps. But it's like trying to hold a kitten; the child struggles and squirms to keep her eyes on Murray. When he disappears around the corner of the house, she breaks free and dashes after him.

"She's sure glommed on to Dad," says Squid.

Hannah isn't sure if it's sadness or amusement in her voice. She can't see Squid's face. "You were the same way whenever you met someone new," she says. "You followed them around just like that."

"Who did *I* ever meet?" asks Squid.

"Oh, come on," says Hannah. "You met technicians, junior keepers . . ." But it's true there weren't very many, and she has to think of others. "The Coast Guard, I guess. And Santa Claus. Oh, and kayakers." Then she stops, almost biting her lip.

"Yeah, I remember," says Squid.

Then Murray comes back down the path, wheeling his wagon behind him. Tatiana is right on his heels, trotting along in her funny walk, one hand on the towbar as though she's the one doing the pulling. Her voice is as shrill and bright as a bird's call. "Look, Mom! I'm helping."

"That's good, Tat," says Squid.

Murray hitches the wagon to the tractor. He asks, "Who wants to ride in the cartie?"

Nobody answers, and that seems to break his heart. He must have said the same thing a thousand times, thinks Hannah, and always Squid would shout, "I do! Oh, I do!" She would leap right from the ground, bouncing like a spring across the grass.

It was too wild for Alastair, too dangerous for anyone but Squid. She loved to stand up in that rickety thing, rocketing down the boardwalk. It was a chariot and she was Ben Hur, and she shouted "Faster!" and "Faster, Dad!" as Hannah held her breath.

But now nobody answers. "Anyone for the cartie?" asks Murray. "Would the Tatty like to ride in the wagon?"

The child gazes up at him, then nods like a jack-in-the-box. She's grinning her wide, funny grin.

"I knew you would!" Murray whisks her up and stands her in the cart. "Hang on," he says. "You hold on to the bar at the front, and if I'm going too fast you just shout 'Whoa!' And don't be scared, wee Tat."

"Dad, please go slow," says Squid.

"Och, who's telling me this?" asks Murray. But he's smiling now, and Tatiana grips the bar as he starts the tractor. It clunks into gear. Tat jolts back, her arms going stiff, as Murray sets off down the path.

She seems to enjoy it, but it's hard for Hannah to tell. From the forest ahead, Tat lets out a cry, and Hannah says, "Something's gone wrong."

"That was a happy shout, I think," says Squid.

But they catch up to Murray, who's parked the tractor and is hurrying back. He snatches something from the boardwalk.

"She dropped her Barney doll," he says, holding it up, then dashes off again.

It takes more than half an hour to walk the boardwalk's length this morning. Squid stops at the places she remembers: at the midden; at the eagles' nest; at the lookout spot above the high north shore where tattered bits of plastic ribbon have turned from red to pink. And with every step Hannah dreads coming to the meadow. But they pass that little splash of green and yellow without stopping, without a comment from either of them. It was in the meadow that Squid was found unconscious, nearly dead.

Now and then they nudge together, then come apart and veer across the boardwalk, in and out of spots of light filtered through the trees.

Murray has the tractor unloaded before they get to the beach. He has spread out the plates and the cutlery down a weathered old log. He's building a fire in a hollow scraped from the sand. Tatiana is watching him intently.

"How's it going?" says Squid.

"Great." Murray takes a bone-dry pine bough and breaks it into twigs. "We're having a terrific conversation here." He arranges the twigs precisely on his moss.

Squid walks around behind Tatiana. She cocks her head. "Really?"

"Oh, yes." He pokes Tat with a twig. "We're going for a swim."

Tat's eyes wrinkle. Her mouth stretches. "Going for a swim," she says.

"It might be too cold for swimming." Squid sits down on the log and pulls Tat back toward her, between her opened legs.

"And you know what else, Tatty?" Murray leans close to her. "Shells!" he says, slowly, bug-eyed.

Tat giggles. "Shells."

"Right you are." He's stacking twigs like teepee poles. "We'll find some periwinkles maybe. Some limpets and some jingle shells. We'll make a pretty necklace."

Murray puts a match to the fire. Out of the moss come gray genies. They bow and stretch, then sink back into orange flames. And onto the crackling twigs go bigger sticks, then driftwood and bark. The smell's like incense to Hannah, wonderfully strong.

"More wood," says Murray. But when he starts up, Squid says, "I'll get it, Dad."

He's clearly surprised. "All right," he says. "Thank you."

It's a lovely, lazy meal that lasts until 9:20, when Murray suddenly remembers the weathers. He gets up, and Tatiana reaches after him, blubbering on the instant.

"Och," he says. "I'll be right back. In the shake of a lamb's tail, wee Tat."

He roars away on the tractor, and Tatiana sits with her back to the water, staring at the forest where the boardwalk winds between the trees. To Hannah she's like a tick without him, like a little red tick frozen as the time goes by. Squid seems content to let her sit there alone, but

Hannah can't bear it. She moves down the beach to comfort the child.

"I've missed this," says Squid. "These cookouts we had."

She's feeding sticks to the fire, thrusting them in like swords. She doesn't seem to care about anything, and Hannah doesn't hesitate now to tell her, "We did it only rarely."

Squid looks up for a moment, then laughs in her unpleasant way. "Oh, not *us*," she says. "God, not you and Dad. Alastair and I did this all the time."

It could be true. They could have done this by themselves early in the mornings.

"And you know what got us started?" She pokes at the fire. "That *Swiss Family Robinson*. Remember how I loved that book?"

"You hated it," says Hannah.

"Oh, Mom, you've forgotten. It was because of that book we went exploring. And that's how we named Almost Nothing Atoll."

"We didn't *have* the book then," says Hannah. "We got it years later."

Squid shakes her head. "We launched the boat right here."

"Yes, I remember that," says Hannah.

"How can you? You didn't even come to see us off."

"What nonsense." Hannah remembers it very well.

It was a gray morning, with rain sure to come. But the day had been picked a week before, and there was no delaying the journey. Alastair and Squid had filled the rowboat with every silly thing they needed; they had made the chart that Alastair said was vital for the trip. That was the word he used. "It's vital," he said. "You can't go *anywhere* without a chart. Not anywhere."

Hannah went down with Murray and helped to launch the boat. Squid and Alastair sat together on the thwart, each with an oar. But the tide was still rising and the boat was overloaded. Murray had chores to do, so he couldn't wait to witness the departure.

It pained the children, she thought, that they had to face her as they rowed away. They were still watching one another when they made their first landfall, on the island across the lagoon. Then Squid called out, "Goodbye, Mom!" And they climbed up, and into the trees.

Hannah walked alone back to the lighthouse. Murray was on his hands and knees at the wailing wall, cutting with a pair of scissors at the blades of grass against the stones, the ones he couldn't reach with the mower. He said, "Are they off?"

"Yes," she said. "Oh, Murray, do you think they're old enough for this?"

"It's past time," he said.

But it was the longest day of their lives, followed by the longest night. Neither of them slept, and in the morning they both hurried to chores that would take them as high from the ground as possible. Murray lit off for the tower, to clean the glass and oil the hinges on the door, he said. But he didn't explain how such simple things could keep him occupied for hours. Hannah got out the ladder and climbed to the roof of the big house. The eaves troughs didn't really need cleaning; Murray had done it not long before, picking out every bit of leaf and grain of shingle before they tainted the drinking water or clogged the pipes leading to the cistern. Then, on their separate perches, she and Murray watched through the morning, though the rain started then, heavy and soaking.

Murray went into the cupola, where he could fiddle with the wiring and wipe the windows and keep himself dry as he worried. But Hannah huddled in the rain, sheltered only by the chimney, like a huge bedraggled stork. She didn't move until the children came up the boardwalk in their yellow coats that flared out from their hips to their knees. The two of them looked like bright-colored bells, their legs for clappers. How proud they were.

They burst through the door just as Hannah came down the stairs in fresh, dry clothes, as Murray appeared from the tower.

"We're back!" shouted Squid. "We've named every island."

"Were you worried?" asked Alastair.

"Not at all," said Murray.

Hannah shook her head. "Why should we worry? You're almost grown up, the two of you now."

⌒

"You didn't even worry," says Squid. She's scraping at the sand with a stick. "We were gone all night, and you didn't even worry."

Hannah sees no point in telling her now. She's sure that Squid wouldn't believe her anyway.

They sit in silence. Squid draws spirals and squares in the sand. Tatiana stares at the forest, and Hannah holds her, trying to remember how it was to hold Squid. Then she laughs, because Squid never stayed still to be held.

"What's so funny?" asks Squid.

"Nothing."

"Well, it's true," says Squid. "We could have drowned, and you didn't even worry."

Hannah sighs. "No, Squid, we *never* worried."

"Maybe you should have," she says.

Hannah strokes Tatiana's pigtails, the hair as dark as Alastair's. If it weren't combed and bound like this it would probably fly apart in the same way, into a clown's mad tangles.

She closes her eyes, suddenly almost in tears. It was Alastair who liked to be held, to be touched and comforted. She bends down her head and rests her cheek on Tatiana's hair.

But the child only squirms, reaching again toward the forest. And a moment later Hannah hears the sound of the tractor purring through the trees. Tatiana tears herself loose and runs to meet Murray as he trots across the sand.

"Hello, Tatty!" he shouts.

He has brought a paper filter for a second pot of coffee. He lays it neatly on the log, and Tat is right there, helping him to smooth it flat, patting with her little hands. "What a helper you are," he says.

Tatiana glows.

"Let's find those jingle shells."

They go off together, across the sand that's heating now, as the sun streams over the trees. They walk, then run, then suddenly drop to the ground, beside a tide pool by the rocks.

"Look at them together," says Hannah. "I haven't seen him run like that in years. She's good for him, Squid."

Squid is building up the fire, blinking in the twirls of smoke.

Hannah says, "Why did you wait so long to bring her home?"

"It isn't home," says Squid.

"Well, whatever it is."

Squid breathes little gasps through the smoke. She shifts sideways, from her knees to her hip. "I was sort of scared," she says.

"Scared? Of your father?"

"No," says Squid. "Not really."

"Of me, then."

"No." Squid waves the smoke away. "The island."

"You were scared of the island?"

"Yes. Sort of. I thought it would—I don't know—take her over, Mom. I was scared she'd *remember* things."

"Like what?"

"Just things." She adjusts the sticks she's put on the fire. "What if she knew where the boardwalk went and where the auklets live? What if she came out on the beach and said, 'I remember all this'?"

"Why would she?" asks Hannah.

Squid shrugs.

"It sounds a bit silly," says Hannah.

"I can see that *now*. I didn't think so then."

Hannah stares along the beach, at Murray and Tat lying on the sand. She imagines that he's lecturing on all the little animals, and she wishes she could hear him. "So why did you come back now?" she asks. But she wonders: *Why, of all times, in the autumn?*

"I had to," says Squid. "I had to see it once more while I can."

Hannah's heart leaps. A hundred fears run through her mind in a moment. "What do you mean?" she says, turning to face her daughter. "What do you mean, while you *can?*"

"I'm going away," says Squid. "*We're* going away, me and Tat." She steps around the fire and sits at Hannah's side. "Mom, I met this guy, this really neat guy, and we're going to live in Australia."

"Forever?"

"For three or four years," says Squid. "But by then . . ."

"We'll be gone," says Hannah. It's not even three years. She knows within ten the number of days until Murray turns sixty-five. And then, she imagines, the Coast Guard will have to come with crowbars to pry him from the island, tearing him loose like a mussel, breaking his byssus at last.

"Don't tell Dad," says Squid.

Hannah scarcely hears her. "Why didn't you bring him, this really neat guy?"

"Mom, don't."

"But why?"

"He left two weeks ago," says Squid. "He's already in Australia."

"Oh, Squid." Hannah sighs. "I should have known it would be something like this. I should have known you were bringing bad news."

"Gee, *thanks*," says Squid. "*I* don't think it's bad news. *I* think . . ."

She doesn't finish. Down the beach, by the shelf of rocks, Murray is springing to his feet. He moves as quickly as a flea; one instant he's squatting by the tide pool with Tatiana, and the next he's upright, hands at his hips. He takes a step backward, then another. Then he wheels around and runs straight toward them.

Squid leaps up, scattering sand. Then Murray stops where he is. He glances back at Tatiana, then calls to Squid and Hannah. "You'll have to see this." He beckons frantically. "You won't believe what she's done."

chapter
ten

*I*T'S NOT A BIG TIDE POOL. IT'S SMALLER THAN a child's wading toy. In its shallow water Hannah sees a sculpin dart from weed to rock, a shore crab glide the other way. The bottom of the pool is covered with small, empty shells, more thickly toward the end where Tatiana holds her hands below the surface.

Murray puts a palm on Tat's shoulder; one of her pigtails brushes his wrist. He bends down until his face is level with hers. He says, "Show them, Tatty."

She doesn't move. Her hands are cupped together, fattened by refractions.

"Come on, Tatty. Open your hands. Do it for Grandpa."

Murray's fingers flex. "Come on, Tat. Please?"

And slowly, like a clamshell, Tatiana's hands fall open.

Hannah has never before seen these animals that are gathered in the creases between Tatiana's fingers, among the ridges that line her small, bent palms. They're tiny things with oversized arms, with claws like a crab's and thin, tapering bodies almost in coils. They don't move; they shelter there.

Squid says, "What are those?"

"Look," says Murray.

Hannah can see it now. But it seems impossible. They're so fragile. All those empty shells in the pool. "Hermit crabs?" she asks.

"Yes," sighs Murray.

And Squid's face turns as pale as the sand. "See, Mom," she says. "It's starting."

"Shhh," says Hannah.

No shells of their own, these little crabs have been living in the cases of dead periwinkles. The sprinkle of empty shells was their armor, their homes. But here they have cast them off, and crawled—so naked and vulnerable—into the safety of Tat's small hands.

"It was just one at first," says Murray. "And then a second, a third. They climbed up over her fingers, over her wrists. They all came, through the water and across the sand."

And she holds them like jewels.

To Hannah it's almost like magic. It's something that Alastair might have done.

He would lie for hours, absolutely still, with a bit of gristle in his fingers. He would be a rock, like a piece of the island, unmindful of the rain or the wind, just for the chance to feed a gull.

And then he would describe in the greatest detail, with the emotion of a preacher, the touch of this wild animal.

"Its feathers were layered," he said one day. He stood in the kitchen, his legs shaking with excitement, crossed close together. "There was a line of white and a line of black and each one was just perfect." His fingers twitched in tiny gestures. "Just perfect, perfect feathers."

When he was twelve, he went after the auklets. He sat for nine straight hours by the mouth of a burrow before Murray brought him away. "Alastair," he said. "Maybe they don't want to be seen."

"Maybe not," said Alastair. "But I think I want what *I* want more than they do."

For three days he sat there, from the moment his chores were finished until just after dawn.

"I think Alastair's gone off the deep end," said Squid. She wouldn't have the patience for that. She'd have to be staked to the ground to stay in one place for nine hours straight.

But on Alastair's fourth day at the burrow, the bird came out. And it wasn't the one he'd expected.

"I saw the baby. It was tipsy and fat," he said in his preachy voice. "It blinked at the sun; it didn't know what it was—what daylight was. I saw it take its very first look at the world. I was the first thing it saw."

"Did it die of shock?" asked Squid.

By the time he reached his teens, Alastair had read every biology text in the house. He craved more, ordering pamphlets and thin little volumes with staggering titles. For Hannah, it was proof the boy should be in school. But Murray outmaneuvered her, and brought the subject up himself.

"You know," he said one morning, "school would be a disappointment for Alastair now. The lad would far outpace any teacher; why, he'd be driven round the bend."

"I just wish he had someone to share with," said Hannah. "That's the sad part. He's so much alone with all that he knows."

Murray's face crumpled.

"Oh," she said, "I didn't mean you. I meant children. Others his age."

"No," said Murray. "Och, you're right. He knows more than me by half."

Murray did his best to catch up. He settled down at night with a stack of pamphlets at his elbow. He nodded off to sleep like that, until the alarm clock woke him at three in the morning, in time to do the weathers.

―――

By then, the four of them overfilled the rowboat. They crowded into it like circus clowns into a silly car, and they brought the gunwales nearly to the water. But still they went drifting over reefs and sand. And through the glass floor they saw a marvelous thing. A nudibranch, one of the giants carried in from the open sea. It was like an orange flame burning through the water, a rippling of tendrils and stalks.

Squid rubbed their breaths from the glass. "Which end is the head?" she asked.

Murray launched into one of his lectures. "The nudibranch," he said. "A snail without a shell. A free spirit wandering wherever the currents take him. He carries no weapons, no armor. He drenches himself in a strong perfume that protects him like a magic potion."

"But where's his head?" asked Squid. "Does he breathe, or what?"

Murray had no answer. He shook his head.

"Those tentacles are called cerata." It was Alastair talking. "The animal breathes through those. That darker part in the center is a crude liver. There can be vast differences between the nudibranchs, even among the solids. MacFarland says the Hermissenda is a voracious killer of other nudibranchs. It slaughters its own kind with the cruelty of a shark."

Squid stared at him. "Huh?" she said.

Alastair blushed horribly.

And poor Murray. His little whimsical lecture sounded pathetic compared to the teachings of Alastair. He said, "I didn't know that. A killer nudibranch?"

Alastair didn't answer. He seemed embarrassed that he knew more than his father.

＿

"You have to let them go," says Murray. He's talking to Tat, about the hermit crabs. But it jolts Hannah back to before.

She told him the same thing. The children, she said, were like balloons in a bottle; if he didn't let them out they could only grow so big, and no bigger.

"I'm doing the best for them I can," he said. "I'm teaching them to think for themselves, to believe in the things they believe. If that's not good enough, then one day they'll tell me so."

"But they won't," said Hannah. "They love you too

much for that. Doesn't the eagle have to *push* the babies out of her nest?"

"Och," he said. "You don't know about eagles."

He hurt her with his quiet anger. She said, "But I know about children. And you have to let them go."

⌒

"They'll die in your hands," says Murray. "They need their freedom, Tat. You'll have to let them go."

Tat doesn't move. She's studying the poor, naked crabs with the same detached interest that she showed for Murray's toys.

The sun comes over her shoulder, dazzling on her hands. The rising tide laps at the far edge of the pool, and ripples run across it.

"Come on," says Murray. "Put them down, Tatty, and we'll find some jingle shells."

She turns her head toward him. "Jingle shells," she says.

"Yes. That's right." Murray puts his big, pink hands into the water. He holds Tat's wrist, and the crabs—frightened—go fleeing. They tumble from her palms like the urchins—so long ago—that had tumbled over the bottom of the sea. They twist and fall, wriggling down to the sand. They race toward the scattered shells, each to its own, and carry them off to the safety of the weeds, to the shelter of the stones.

Hannah looks up, and Squid is gone. She's back at the fire, scattering the sticks, kicking them across the sand. Hannah stands by the pool for a moment, watching Murray and Tat go off along the curve of beach, one so big and one so small. Now and then they crouch, and dabble in the sand. Hannah wishes she could join them, but she goes to Squid instead. She starts packing away the breakfast things.

Squid is scooping sand on the coals, smothering the last of the flames. The smell is hot and bitter. "I'm leaving on the next boat," she says.

"That's a month from now, and you know it," says Hannah.

"Well, maybe one will come sooner." Squid stamps over the mound of sand. "As soon as one comes, I'm going."

"You'll break your father's heart," says Hannah.

"Well, he broke mine."

"Squid!"

"He did. He killed Alastair. And I'm not going to let him get Tat."

"What a terrible thing to say. You make him sound like Bluebeard."

Squid's laugh is almost cruel. She keeps bustling around, gathering the aluminum foil that had wrapped the potatoes. She finds Tatiana's Barbie doll and sits it upright on the sand. She never looks at Hannah. "It's already inside her."

"The island?"

"Yes."

"Well, how could it not be? It's all you ever knew," says Hannah. "You've probably told her everything about it."

"Maybe Dad's right. She *has* come home."

"And what's wrong with that?"

"I don't want it to *be* her home." Squid crushes the foil

into a ball and jams it in the bucket. "If she stays any longer something awful will happen. I know it will."

The sun is hot, the sand baking in its whiteness. Hannah is tired of arguing. "Fine," she says. "But you'll have to tell Murray you're leaving. You'll have to tell him about Australia."

"I will."

"Today," says Hannah. "It isn't fair to let him think he's got a grandchild now, only to whisk her away forever."

"It's his own fault," she says.

"Oh, grow up, Squid!"

"Well, it is, Mom. You saw what he did to Alastair."

He drowned. Hannah has told herself over and over that it might have been an accident. She has tried to make herself believe that, in the end, no one could save him. He went out on a sea of rolling black hills, under a sky that was bright with stars. He went out past the rocks and out past the reefs, paddling on with his back to the light. He paddled so far that no one would hear him if, in his drowning, he shouted for help.

From the bridge she saw the kayak. It was such a bright red in the morning, rocking on the waves with a bubble of air, and a slap, as the cockpit went in and out of the water. It was a thin, red smear, like bright-painted lips on the waves. But she could see from the bridge that it was upside down. And she knew right away; Alastair was gone.

Squid was with her. They had walked together to the tower, slowly there and slowly back. She remembers how they paused at the middle of the bridge, over the highest part of the gulf, and put their weight on the railing. Through her elbows and her shoulders, she could feel the wood shake as the swells boomed through the gully below them.

The tide was ebbing and the starfish clung to the rock like orange asterisks. The water rose over them and poured away, draining through the barnacles with the sizzling sound of fat in a frying pan. She watched the waves roll in and thought, again, how they were eating at the island, each one taking a tiny particle that reduced Murray's world by an atom. Then Squid clutched her arm. "Mom," she said. "Look."

The kayak rocked on each crest and turned as it slid to each trough. It came toward them and veered away, borne by the ebb past the gray rocks at the tower, drawn down the passage where the sand, in the sun, looked like gold in the water. It bumped against the concrete steps, lifting on a swell that dropped away to leave one end stranded on the concrete. It rocked far on its side and then, lifted again, went along on its way toward the beach at the end.

She called for Murray. She shrieked his name. Squid shouted too, and they frightened the gulls that swirled up from the surf, taking their cries in a high, winding circle.

Murray came with a wrench in his hand. He came at a run, over the grass, a look of terrible fear on his face. He paused at the cliffs, and he panicked. He ran down the steps, down the chipped-away stairs to the sea. And at the bottom he kept running, up to his knees and his thighs, up to his waist, and the swell rose over his shoulders. He swam out to the kayak and groped underneath it. He rolled it upright and threw himself across the cockpit. On his waist and his elbows, the water pouring from him in silvery rivers, he looked frantically around him. Then he put back his head and shouted one word into that great emptiness of the sea and the islands.

"Alastair!" he shouted.

And the surf boomed on the rocks, eating at a world that had shrunk on an instant to nothing.

"Alastair wouldn't have been happy anywhere," says Hannah. "If he had got everything he wanted, he *still* wouldn't have been happy."

At last Squid looks at her. "You don't know the things he told me."

"No." And she doesn't *want* to know.

"I tried to help him, Mom." Squid sits down on a log. She puts her hands to her face. "I did everything I could, and it just turned rotten in the end. I did the wrong things, I think."

"We all felt like that." She stands as close as she dares to her daughter. "We should have seen it coming."

At thirteen he was a dreamy, distant child. He asked for a flute for Christmas, but not for a music book. "I don't want a book," he said. "I want to play from my heart, not from a splatter of dots on a page."

He blew across the mouthpiece and pressed the keys. Tootling, Murray called it. Alastair made bird sounds, whale sounds; he didn't make music.

He started going off by himself, often in the kayak.

Even Squid didn't know where he went, and she hated him for that.

"I could kill him," she said. "He makes me so mad."

Hannah told her, "He's going through a phase." She said, "He needs some privacy."

And Squid asked: "What if he paddles away? What if he just keeps going and never comes back? The stupid moron, he'll be down in Vancouver before he knows he's away."

"He won't leave you," said Hannah. "One day, I'm sure, the two of you will live as neighbors somewhere in the city."

That was the way she saw it. Alastair would tear himself from the island. Squid would follow a few months later. It would be impossible for them to live more than an hour apart.

She tried to prepare Murray for that, but of course he wouldn't listen. "Och, they'll never leave," he said. "We're too much of a unit for that."

"A unit?" she said. "We're drifting apart. We'll be at each other's throats if it goes on like this."

And Murray said, "Alastair will be the keeper after me. Squid will catch the eye of one of those Coast Guard types. We'll build her another house where she can bring up her children."

She gaped at him. He had no idea that everyone but him was already thinking of leaving.

"I've picked out a spot," he said. He was splicing new lines for the flag halyards, and he put down his tape and his fids. "Come on and I'll show you," he said.

It was a gusty day and the whirligigs rattled, then

stopped. She followed Murray past the wooden lady at the pump, past the airplane that flapped its wings as they went by, like a bird they had startled, past the galloping horse and into the forest.

He veered off the boardwalk and went close to the cliffs. There was a circle of moss in a clearing. He said, "This is the place. Look at the view that they'll have."

She looked down the cliffs and across the channel. She saw a spot of bright red out on the reefs, tossed by the white of the surf. It was Alastair, paddling the kayak, heading straight out as the waves crashed on the rocks and shattered into feathery plumes. And then she saw the orcas, the killer whales, beyond him. Their fins flashed through the water, black scythes cutting thin little furrows. They spouted and breached. Alastair rode in a swell until she could see nothing but his head, and his hands with the paddle. Then the wave passed and he soared up on its green back, the kayak shedding water. The whales swam behind and before him, in a shimmering mist of breath.

"This will be the living room here," Murray was saying. He had marked out the place with stakes and string and crimson ribbons of plastic. "They'll have the best view on the island. The kitchen there; the bedrooms at the back."

Alastair kept paddling. Leaning forward, he dragged himself through the water. He vanished in the trough, then rose again on the next wave. The whales went in circles around him.

"I suspect she'll have two children," said Murray. "So we'd better plan three bedrooms right off the bat. And maybe a study—what do you think?—where she can work with her shells and her jewelry."

"It won't happen," she said. "She won't stay."

"Of course she will." Murray came up through the moss and stood at the edge of the cliff. "Och, she might go away; I'll grant you that. They both might go away for a while. But they'll see what the world is like soon enough, and they'll be home before the year is out. Mark my words, Hannah. They can't stay away from the island."

Alastair turned his kayak into the waves. They rolled below him, tilting him up their white-streaked faces, up their beards of foam, and he seesawed on the crests and went sliding down again. He put away his paddle and took up his flute instead, and the music that he made came to her in bits, in little squeals and shrieks that sounded to Hannah like voices in panic.

"Look at him there," said Murray. "Where else could he do that? Why would he ever want to leave?"

She didn't answer. It seemed to her that he'd left already.

⌐~

"Poor Alastair," says Hannah.

Squid mumbles something that Hannah can't hear. Squid reaches out and, when Hannah steps closer, takes hold of her dress, squeezing big lumps in her fists.

"He couldn't bear to go, and he couldn't bear to stay," says Hannah. She touches Squid's shoulders. "But he loved you more than anyone."

Squid groans.

"I blamed your father; God knows I did. I blamed myself and him." She holds on to Squid with a fierceness. "But don't think you had anything to do with it. You kept him alive."

Squid pulls herself away. She wipes her nose with the back of her hand, then gets to her feet and shakes sand from her blouse and her jeans.

"I'm going up to the house," she says. "Okay, Mom? I just want to go up to the house by myself."

chapter
eleven

September 13. *They say that drowning is an easy way to die. They say that there's a moment of panic and a moment of pain and after that there's pleasure. You try to breathe but you can't. Your body won't let you. You go back through your life, and into a brightness of light. And at the end you're happy and fearless.*

So why do they scream? Why do they fight and struggle so much? Why do they call for their mothers?

Squid lies on the bed in Alastair's room. Stretched out on her stomach, her feet on his pillow, she props her chin on her left hand, and turns through the pages of Alastair's book. In the pages, and in her mind, he's thirteen years old again.

Last night we heard men drowning.

She remembers that day, the bleakest day in a long, bleak autumn. It brought a storm worse than any she had known and any that would follow. It was seven months before the *Odd Fellow* sank.

All through the morning, Murray tapped and tapped at the barometer, watching the pointer swing backward on the dial nearly as fast as a second hand moves. The clouds gathered in heaps, boiling dark tendrils as they swept up from the south. The wind rose with a fury that surprised even Murray. At noon it shrieked through the trees. At dusk it snatched the wooden lady from her pump and sent Old Glory galloping over the grass.

That evening, Alastair polished his oil-burning lantern and trimmed the wick. The chimney—thin as paper—tingled with a musical hum as each gust of wind howled at the side of the house. He set the lantern on his windowsill with a matchbook beside it, the cover open, one match torn out and left lying across the striker.

"If the beacon goes out," he told her, "I want to be ready."

But Murray kept them all together in the big house. He insisted on that, then insisted on going to the tower himself, though it wasn't his turn for the weathers. He wore his oilskins and a black, floppy sou'wester. He called his boots Wellingtons. "Och, I'll be needing my Wellingtons," he said. "The lawn's like an ocean out there."

He was gone nearly an hour before they saw him—bent and staggering—fight his way back against the wind. A shrieking gust and a spray of cold rain came in behind him when he opened the door. His sou'wester had been torn from his head. His eyes, half blinded by spray, were as red as Christmas balls.

"The waves are breaking right over the bridge," he

said. "I've seen nothing like it. Nothing half so bad as this."

The surf boomed and roared against the rocks. The bronze bell rang on the porch as a gust of wind pushed on the clapper.

"I thought I might get carried away," said Murray. He hung his coat on a peg, and his shoulders were wet underneath. He pulled at his Wellingtons. "The flag's gone. Nothing but tatters. The gusts are too strong for the meter to read, and it's getting worse all the time."

His feet came from his boots with a long, sucking squelch, and his woolen socks—sodden with water—drooped from his toes. A puddle spread around him. "I need a towel," he said. "Hannah, can you fetch me a towel?"

Alastair squinted through the window. "Is the light still on?" he asked.

"Och, I didn't look up," said Murray.

But it was. Spray flew white as snow through the beacon's twirling arms.

At eleven o'clock, Squid was in the kitchen with Alastair. The room was kept dark so that they could see through the big, south-facing window. A gust shook the house; the bell rang on the porch—a sharp, tingling peal. And Squid saw a flare sputter up into the rain and the wind, a thin line of red like an exclamation mark etched on the black of the pane.

Alastair went right to the window. He pressed his hands on the glass and leaned against it. He held his glasses in his hands, blinking his wet, gloomy eyes. "I wish I could see," he said. "Oh, I wish I could see."

"Dad!" shouted Squid. "Mom!" They came together into the kitchen. Rain slammed at the window, warping the glass, for an instant turning it white.

"Stand back from there!" said Murray. "That window's next to go."

Water went coursing down the glass, and another flare rose from the storm, swimming up through the ripples as the window shivered and crackled.

"Good lord," said Murray. "There really is someone out there."

Again, to Squid, it looked like an exclamation mark. And she saw a terrible sadness in the faintness of it, the futility. A scream for help without a sound.

Murray switched on the radio, the VHF. He unclipped the microphone from the little chrome holder. The cord twisted in coils round his wrist. From the speaker came a voice, a man's voice that was surprisingly calm, though strange from the fear at the edge of it. He was saying, over and over, as steady as a machine, "Mayday, mayday, mayday."

"Let go of the key," said Murray, softly. "I can't answer you, man, as long as you're holding the key."

Again the bell rang as they all faced the window, as the glass bulged toward them. The radio was over the sink, fixed under the cupboards. And the voice filled the room with its urgency.

"Mayday, mayday, mayday!"

"Let go of the key," said Murray again.

At last the man did. And instantly another voice answered. It was deep and soothing, a God-like sound. "The vessel calling mayday," it said. "This is Prince Rupert Coast Guard radio."

There was a strength in that voice. It brought a calm-ness and a sense of trust, and Squid closed her eyes for a moment and let out a small sigh. That voice commanded a tranquility from the man on the boat, and asked, "What is the nature of your emergency?"

The boat, a troller named *Cape Caution*, was taking on water faster than the pumps could get it out. The boards that covered the cockpit had been torn away in the storm, and now the waves—rolling up from the stern—tumbled over the transom, pouring hundreds of gallons into the hull.

Murray replaced the microphone in its clip. He spoke straight at the window, as though his voice could carry clear across the sea. "Turn around, man. Go *into* the waves." Hannah, close beside him, held on to his arm.

Then the God-like voice asked, "What is your posi-tion?"

The boat was just a few miles from Lizzie Island. It was making for the shelter of its sand and trees, heading for the beacon. Just a few miles to go, but right to leeward, chased by waves that hammered it down, that climbed aboard to sink it.

There were three people on board, the fisherman said. Himself, and two of his sons.

"Do you have a lifeboat?" asked the Coast Guard.

"No, sir," said the fisherman.

"Do you have survival suits?" There was no answer. Again the Coast Guard asked, "Do you have survival suits?"

And the man answered, "One. We only have one."

"Oh, God," said Hannah. She leaned her head on Murray's shoulder. "Oh, Murray, the poor man."

What would he do? wondered Squid. What would anyone do? She saw the father tearing open the bag, hauling
from it this big orange thing like a man without flesh. He
throws it down on the deck. "Put it on!" he commands.
But who does he look at? Which of his sons does he save?
Do they fight to see who gets it, this one little chance to
survive? Does son battle with son? Son against father? Or
do they all stare at this thing lying on the deck and shout
at one another, "You put it on!" Would the horror be
greater, or less, if you were the one in the suit?

"For heaven's sake," said Murray. "*Someone* put it on."

The Coast Guard sent a cutter. The voice like God
said it would get there in ninety minutes.

"Too late," said Murray. "That boat will either be here
or be gone."

For half an hour the Coast Guard coaxed the troller
along. And the McCraes, in the kitchen, listened as the
fisherman came toward them. In the background of his radio they heard a motor thrumming, and the whine of the
wind in his rigging. They heard the fear come to his voice,
leave it again, and return. It washed over him with the
regularity of each giant wave.

"The stabilizers won't stay in the water," he said. "I
can't see the deck anymore."

Calm and deep, the voice asked, "Are you making
progress?"

"We can see the island. We can see the houses on the
island."

"Turn around, man," said Murray.

"How could he?" said Squid. She still stared at the
window, at the blackness. "He's too close to go back."

For a long time, the fisherman didn't talk. A tree shattered outside. The gust of wind rushed on through the forest with a sound like tearing cloth, howled along the roof, and the bell rang twice as rain thundered on the shingles like cattle hooves. In the kitchen, Squid saw, Murray and Hannah and Alastair were all leaning forward, still facing the window.

"*Cape Caution,*" said the Coast Guard, and waited for an answer. "*Cape Caution.*" Another long silence. "*Cape Caution,* this is Prince Rupert Coast Guard radio."

"They're gone," said Murray softly.

"No," said Hannah. "They've come so close. They *have* to make it now."

"*Cape Caution. Cape Caution.*"

Alastair rubbed his hands together. "Oh please, God," he whispered.

"*Cape Caution. Cape Caution.*"

Murray reached for the radio switch. But his hand gave a jerk as the fisherman's voice leapt from the speaker. It was so matter-of-fact.

"The engine's gone; the water's over the floor." Behind him was a crashing sound, a breaking of the timbers. And then the screaming started. One voice, and then three, all of them hollering and screaming. It lasted only an instant, and then it was quiet again.

There was only a bleating, useless voice asking, "*Cape Caution? Cape Caution?*"

The cutter arrived just after midnight. It fired white flares into the storm, a stream of flares that sizzled and popped, making patches out on the ocean. Wreckage came ashore, but never a body. And never a survival suit.

September 14. *I keep wondering. What would I do if that was me on the boat—me and Squid and Dad—and we only had one survival suit? The best thing, really, would be for Dad to put it on. And then he could hold us both and keep us out of the water. Dad could float for a long, long time. But it would never happen that way. Who would it be best to save, I wonder. Squid who's youngest, or Dad who's oldest. It would have to be one or the other.*

September 15. *What difference does it make if you live to be ninety or only nineteen? Why is it so awful if a baby dies, but not an old, old man? They'll both be dead for the same length of time. I think there must be a heaven to go to that sort of evens things out. After all, if I was a tortoise I'd live a hundred years, but if I was a mayfly I would be alive for just one day. And then, after millions of years in heaven, I'd be the same age either way. I think I've got it figured out. But Squid says it's wrong.*

He came to her with his ideas. He'd made a graph that showed all of time, a trillion billion years in a line across the page. At the left side was the start of the world, and half an inch later he'd made a little mark and labeled it "Today." Crowded to the right of that were a lot of little marks that made one giant smudge.

"What's all that?" she asked.

"Lifetimes," said Alastair, and told her about the mayfly and the tortoise. "See?" he said. "If you look at all the time in heaven they're just the same age in the end."

She said, "But would you rather be the tortoise or the fly?"

"It doesn't matter," he said, breathing through his nose. "That's what I'm trying to tell you."

She pointed at the page. "So what's the lifetime here for idiots?"

September 16. *I've decided to read the Bible. I snuck it up to my room and started reading a little bit every night. Genesis was pretty good, but I can't figure out where all the people in the valleys came from if God only made Adam and Eve. I'm praying for Mom. I wish she was happier. And I'm praying that my eyes get strong. I guess I should really just scrunch up my glasses. But I don't have enough faith for that yet.*

She heard him praying at night, his quiet voice going on and on. He asked her strange questions: "How much rain do you think it would take to cover Lizzie Island? How big is a cubit, anyway?" And, slowly, he lapsed into the first of his times of lonely brooding.

He looked smaller because he was always hunched over. All four of them could be squashed into one little room, but she could look at Alastair and think he was all alone. She would walk with him down the boardwalk, and suddenly he would turn and sprint off through the trees.

In the days that followed the storm, they replaced battered shingles torn from the roof, then cleared the trees blown down on the boardwalk. Murray worked the chain saw in a cloud of oily smoke as the sawdust flew against his legs. Then he turned off the clattering engine and said, "That's enough for today," and Alastair was gone before the sentence was finished.

"We have to give the lad some time," said Murray,

later, while they sat on the grass as he sharpened the saw. Murray would never put away a tool that was dirty or dull.

"How much time?" asked Squid.

Murray shrugged. He sat with the chain saw between his legs, filing at the teeth. "He's got to sort things out. Things he's never fathomed."

"And what if he can't?" said Hannah. She'd put on a dress that was printed with flowers. A honeybee buzzed around her, darting in and out toward the gaudy colors on the cloth.

Squid lay between her parents, on her stomach on the grass.

"Well, he has to," said Murray. "It's as simple as that." The file rasped across the teeth, three strokes to each one. Squid hated the sound it made.

"When I was a boy," said Murray, "there was an explosion in the mine. For two days we didn't know who was alive and who was dead, and my father was down there all the time." He wiped his forehead, rubbing at the spot above his nose. "I remember the women, how they waited for news. And I remember the searchers coming up with their faces all black."

He tested the sawteeth with his thumb. "There were six men trapped down there. Three came out alive—my father among them—and three were carried out dead. Another fellow—I can't remember his name—he should have been with them, but he wasn't. That morning he'd woken up and decided that he wouldn't go down in the mine that day. And he never went down again."

"Who could blame him?" asked Hannah.

"It's not the point," said Murray. "He came to believe

that he *was* down there, that seven men went down to the mine. He believed that the explosion left him trapped and dying. He could see it, you understand; he could see himself buried in rubble, and he could hear himself screaming for help. And this is what he decided." Murray pulled the file through his fingers and wiped off a silvery sludge. He moved the chain along, and started filing again. "Salvador, that was his name. He was a huge man. He decided that he had begged God not to let him die, to give him another chance if he made himself a better man. And he came to believe that God had answered the prayer, and when he woke up that morning and didn't go to work it was because time had been set back to keep him from dying."

Hannah didn't speak for a moment, and then she laughed with a nervous giggle. "Good heavens," she said.

"Well," said Murray. "My father said that Salvador was a lazy sod who didn't go to work two days out of every month at any rate. He said, and I remember this very clearly"—Murray held up the file like a wand—"he said, 'Och, he wasna the only one beggin' for mercy then, but time didna go backwards for us.'"

Squid dug her toes in the grass. "Did your dad go back to work?" she asked.

"For a while," said Murray. "Don't do that, Squid; you'll make holes."

She rolled lazily onto her back. "So, what does this have to do with Alastair?"

"Och, don't you see?" he said. "What a person thinks of things isn't worth a tinker's dam. Surely there's no fathoming the ways of the world, so why bother trying? It's living that matters. It's life that's important."

He put down the file and pushed away the saw. He stood up and said, "I think I'll tell that story to Alastair. Where has he gone, do you think?"

"To the beach," said Squid. "He just sits by the water."

Murray started off. "Wait," said Hannah. "Did Salvador become a better man?"

"Och, he was a pain in the neck after that. He was nutty as a fruitcake."

September 20. *Dad came down to the beach and told me a story. I didn't see much point to it. But I felt sorry for him, the way that he's worried about me, and I went with him back to the house.*

Squid remembers how Murray glowed as he came up the boardwalk with Alastair. She remembers being so glad to see her brother that she laughed and shouted out, "Well, look who's alive."

He came trudging behind Murray, his hair even wilder than usual.

"We thought you were dead," cried Squid. "We were scared to go look."

Hannah shot her an awful stare that stunned her into silence.

Alastair stared at them, his face all drawn and ghastly. "I'm sorry if I worried you," he said. "I felt like being alone."

Squid turned from face to face. "Isn't anyone going to ask him what he's been doing?"

"I'm sure if Alastair wants to tell us that, he'll do so in his own good time," said Hannah primly. Then Murray clapped his hands and shouted, "Right! Let's break into teams for a badminton game."

They played all afternoon, the men against the girls. Alastair stumbled about, swatting at the air, and they laughed and laughed together.

Then winter settled in, and it was much like all the winters before. They worked and they played, and Murray lectured on animals, but Alastair was never quite the same. They would catch him sometimes just staring at the sea, watching the waves, standing alone on a rock as the tide rose around him.

Squid turns through the pages.

December 3. *Mom and Dad look at me in funny ways, watching me all the time. They look at me with that sort of squint they use at birthdays, when a balloon is blown so big it's just about to pop.*

I don't know what's wrong with me. I just want to crawl into a burrow, like an auklet or an otter, and stay there and never come out.

chapter twelve

IN MIDAFTERNOON, HANNAH SETS A LUNCH on the lawn. Sockeye salmon, spread in thick swaths on the toast, is nearly the color of raspberries. On half the slices, it's speckled with relish, tiny chunks of green and yellow mixed the way that Squid would do it, in her childhood. In those days Squid called it puke. "Let's have puke sandwiches," she would say, much to Murray's disgust.

Hannah stands, looking down, pleased with the colors on Murray's perfect grass, her bright yellow plates crowded with carrots and green peppers and wedges—like smiles—of red tomato. It's the sort of thing Alastair would have noticed, and commented on, sometimes pecking a kiss on her cheek. "Looks great, Mom," he would tell her.

But Murray, of course, doesn't notice. He comes with Tatiana toddling along at his heels. He keeps looking back. "There's a good girl. Och, you're a wee little walker." They sit together, and Murray pulls one plate toward him.

"Where's Squid?" asks Hannah.

"She's coming," he says. "She told me so—shouting through the door of the small house. She wouldn't let me in."

"Maybe she's changing."

"Let's hope so," says Murray, only half to himself. He takes a carrot from the plate and offers it to Tatiana. She shakes her head, pulling away. She does the same with the peppers, the same with the toast. "You have to eat," he tells her. "You want to grow up big and strong, you have to eat, little Tat."

He does funny things with the food, things he hasn't done since Squid was two years old. He turns the carrots into airplanes, zooming them high, puttering with his lips the sound of propellers. Jets would be too advanced for Murray. "Open the hangar," he says.

Tatiana's eyes follow the carrots, crossing comically as they whiz past her nose. But she doesn't eat. She only watches the carrots, and gazes at Murray.

She has taken to him in such a powerful way that Hannah feels frightened. Someone has to be hurt in the end, and if it isn't Murray it will be this odd little girl, as fragile as a soap bubble. Hannah turns away, feeling lonely there beside them.

But suddenly, Tatiana laughs. Murray has carrot sticks stuffed in his nostrils, a coil of green pepper coming out from his mouth like a snake's tongue. He's holding tomato slices over his eyebrows, and underneath he looks so happy, so young, so much like a boy in his bush of bright hair.

Hannah almost wishes that Squid would stay on the island, that she would abandon her "really neat guy" and settle on Lizzie again. She wants to ask Murray what he thinks; the words are right in her mouth: *Oh, Murray, wouldn't it be nice if she stayed?* But she won't let them out, and she feels wicked for that. She feels old and bitter, ugly inside.

<hr />

Squid has put on a dress that bares her shoulders and arms, and most of her legs. She announces herself with a shout, then comes over the grass like a nymph from a mist. Her feet, without shoes, seem to walk on only the tips of the stems, and her dress floats all around her like rippling steam.

It seems impossible that she was once seven years old, coming home all covered in burrs. Somehow, inside her, is the child who played at soldiers with skunk cabbage heads for grenades, who crawled into otter dens to see what was there, and stood on her head like a barnacle. How had they made her this way? How, on a rock in the middle of nowhere, had they taught her to be a lady?

Her arms swing wide, her head tosses and sways. But ten yards away she starts to run, and there's the girl again. She skips over the grass, laughing with delight. She sees the plates and says, "Oh, boy. Puke for lunch. I haven't had puke in years."

"Och," says Murray.

She folds herself onto the grass. She takes two slices of toast.

"Tat won't eat," says Murray.

"No wonder." Squid holds her palm under her mouth, catching the globs of sockeye and relish that ooze from the sides of the bread. "You haven't cut her toast into fingers."

"Oh, that's ridiculous," says Hannah. "A child that age."

But Murray says, "So that's the trick, is it?" And he lifts his hip from the grass to take out his knife. He opens the blade and patiently slices the toast into strips.

At last the child eats, finger after finger. And Murray methodically cuts up the carrots and cuts up the peppers. Tatiana hums to herself, rocking on the grass.

The ravens come, one then two, and half a dozen. They flutter down on wings that whistle, then stand nearby, black and shiny, waiting there like butlers. They cock their heads and utter warbly croaks through open beaks, and Hannah tosses toast toward them.

"They don't often come as close as this anymore," says Murray. He turns his head away, covering his mouth with a hand, picking at his big teeth with a fingernail.

"Alastair would have them feeding from his hand," says Hannah. And then she stops, seeing the look on her daughter's face.

Murray doesn't notice; he's staring at the sea. "I think the whale's out there," he says.

They all turn to look, out past the tower, off to the south. They watch and wait, and then a spout appears, a little jet of fog. And a black shape rises from the water, bulges up and sinks again.

The sun is not as bright as it was an hour ago. High, hazy clouds are moving in from the west. The sea is a brilliant blue, rolling with a gentle swell. And the whale's nearly a mile offshore, huffing breaths over that flat, heaving plain. They see his back, and once his flukes. He's swimming toward the island.

Even Tatiana stands to watch him. A hand on Murray's shoulder, she stretches up to see.

"We should row out there," says Murray.

"Yes," says Squid. She straightens out her gold-tanned legs.

"Wait," says Hannah. "We've got the food. The dishes." She's still nervous at the thought of being too close to whales in a small and aging boat. She wishes that Murray would go, and Tatiana, that Squid would stay to talk things out, to finish what they've started. But already the dishes are being gathered and Squid is on her feet.

Tatiana seems to have sensed adventure, and her sweet little face is bright with pleasure.

⁓

The boat has sat so long at the edge of the forest that it's filled with old, dead leaves and pinkish crab shells brought there by the otters. Murray tips it onto its side and hammers on the bottom to knock away debris. He drags it down to the water and they climb into their favorite places, Squid—with Tat—in front, Hannah in the little seat that faces Murray.

Even now his arm muscles ripple and bulge as he rows, his calves swell with the motion. He pulls on the oars with a steady, thumping rhythm, driving the boat across the lagoon, out through the gap and past the mooring buoy. The blades of the oars make whirlpools in the water, a trail of them like footprints.

Through the glass at her feet, Hannah sees a forest of kelp drop to a blue darkness. An orange jellyfish rolls by, tendrils stirred by the oars. Years ago, Murray would have stopped here. "The jellyfish," he would have said. "A mindless simpleton with no sense of direction. He hardly knows up from down."

But now he keeps rowing. His face takes on a reddish brightness. His cheeks puff out, and he glances over his shoulder to see how far he has to go.

Hannah stares at the glass. She doesn't want to look at Almost Nothing Atoll and keeps her head down until she feels the boat lift on a swell, and knows they've gone past the tower. She consoles herself with a thought: It won't be a long trip. They've got the weathers to do at half past three.

From the bow comes Squid's shout. "She blows!"

"Where-away?" says Murray, sweat on his forehead.

How easily they've slipped back through the years.

"Straight ahead, Dad."

Murray keeps rowing. The oars thud and creak as the boat rises sluggishly up, then wallows back down.

"A bit to the left," says Squid. "Oh! She blows!"

Tatiana wriggles around, trying to stand up. "Sit still!" says Squid. Then, "Flukes up! She's sounding."

It takes a moment for the noise to come across the water: the slap of a tail; the rush of water. Murray stops rowing. He pulls the oars from the rowlocks and lays them on the seats. It could be half an hour before the whale rises again.

"Whale," says Tat, in that odd little voice.

"Hush." Squid touches her arm.

"Whale," says Tat, insistent.

And the boat vibrates.

There's a sound coming up through the wood and the

frames, a creak like door hinges. Then another, as though someone has tossed sand at the planking. Squid drops her hand into the water. Hannah swallows her fear; they've done this before, she remembers.

"I can feel it," says Squid. "I can feel it!" And again Hannah hears the sound of tossing sand.

So the whale has found them. Its sonar washes over the boat. Somewhere below this empty sea, a thing fifty feet long is turning toward them.

The sound loudens and quickens. In their sockets, the oarlocks vibrate. And then, close alongside, the whale comes sliding from the sea. A mound of brownish skin, bumps and warts. It rises up in silence, slow and majestic. The crack of a mouth, the blowholes on a sculptured base. They open, and the breath comes out, warm and fetid, mist rising in a cloud, raining down. The sound is a hollow clap. And the whale arches, higher than their heads, arches as the water pours off, gliding forward and down, its hump of a fin showing before it sinks again under the swells.

The wave rocks the boat.

"Holy shit," says Squid. Hannah sees Murray wince.

The sound fades. Way off by the island, the whale spouts again. But nobody moves; nobody can.

Tatiana turns her bright, squinted eyes right toward Hannah. Her grin puffs up her cheeks like a squirrel's. She claps her hands together, then slams them to her chest. And suddenly she squeals.

It's a hooting, mournful sound—a wonderful sound. And it comes back to her through the thin bottom of Murray's boat, this caroling of bubbles and bells, this magical singing of whales.

Hannah stares at the glass floor of a boat that's more than a decade old. An eye: a huge, bulging eye. It's what she expects to see on the other side, an eye full of the blues and greens of the oceans, a pupil deep as an abyss.

And now it's what she *wants* to see. She wants to see it pass below the boat, fifty feet of it rolling from back to belly, its graceful fins flapping like wings, a trail of bubbles floating up to pop against the glass.

But she sees only water.

They sit for a long time. The clouds slowly thicken, paling the sun. Then Murray, without a word, jams the oars into place. The blades sweep around in long, lazy arcs. And he rows the boat home with tears on his cheeks.

There hasn't been a humpback near the island since the autumn that Alastair died. Murray and Hannah and Squid rowed out to see them; Squid shouted, "She blows!" And the songs of the whales tickled the boat. Alastair wasn't there; he was off by himself in the kayak.

There were two whales and they swam close together, so close their flippers must have touched. They came to the surface together, the sound of their breaths making only one clap. For Hannah, the whales made her think of Alastair and Squid, the way they used to be but no longer were.

The humpbacks stayed much longer than usual. They arrived, that year, in the summer, moved on for a while, and returned. Whenever he saw them, Alastair would take his flute and his notebook and paddle off in the kayak.

Often she saw him, either wedged in that long narrow boat or sprawled on the rocks of Almost Nothing Atoll.

Not once in that time did she try to go after him. But Murray did. And Alastair climbed into the kayak and—pretending not to see—went off chasing the whales.

But one afternoon he didn't go after them. Hannah was in the kitchen when he stopped at the big house instead. Murray was putting new putty around the huge front window. Hannah heard them talking.

"Dad?" said Alastair. "Do you think whales have a language?"

There was a tap as Murray put his putty knife onto the sill. The porch shook as he crossed it; she imagined that they sat on the steps.

"Language is very complex," Murray said. "It implies words, and structure. I'm sure whales communicate, but I doubt you'd call it a language."

Alastair said, "I think that it is."

"Oh?" said Murray.

"I've heard them. Even without the hydrophone. The kayak, it's like a sound chamber. I've heard them talk to each other."

Murray grunted. "You've heard them make sounds to each other," he said.

"No, it's more than that." There was an anguish in Alastair's voice. "Dad, I'd like to study it."

"Good," said Murray. "We'll order some books. Just give me some titles and—"

"Not from books, Dad." He was frustrated now. "I'd need a spectrograph, hydrophones. A sound editor."

"We can get those things."

"I'd want to be where the whales are."

"Oh," said Murray. "Oh, I see."

"I'll let you off here," says Murray. Already he's nudging the boat up to the base of the concrete steps. "No sense in you walking clear over the island."

Squid laughs. "Too hard to row?" she asks.

"Well, there is that," he says. "But, och, if you like—"

"No," says Hannah. "This is fine." He's sweating now, but too proud to say he's had enough. She reaches out for the step, clutching at seaweed and kelp. Murray pushes with the oars, holding the boat in place, and she clambers out. Without her weight, the boat tips forward.

"Hey!" says Squid.

Hannah holds the transom in place. "Come on, Tatiana," she says. "We're going to go up the stairs."

But Tatiana won't move. When Squid picks her up by the waist, she clings to the bow, kicking her feet.

"Stop that!" says Squid. "You're making a scene."

"She's rocking the boat, right enough," says Murray. He steadies it with sweeps of the oars as Squid wrestles behind him with Tatiana. "Och, just leave the wee thing; she's no bother to me."

"Fine!" says Squid. "You *stay* here," she tells Tat, instantly mad. She clambers past Murray, stepping over the oars. In her hurry she uses his head for a handhold, scrunching it sideways. She doesn't look back but goes straight up the stairs, glowering at Hannah as she passes.

"Go slowly," Hannah tells Murray. She sends the boat off with a push and climbs up after Squid, who waits at the top with her hands on her hips.

"This really bugs me," says Squid.

"What?"

"The way Dad's taking over."

"Now, don't blame your father. It's Tatiana who wanted to stay."

"But he didn't make her get out."

"Neither did you."

Squid pouts—the child again. "If Dad had told her to, she would have. She does anything for Dad."

"Yes, she loves him," says Hannah.

"If she stayed on the island, Dad would spoil her rotten."

"Hardly!" says Hannah. "He would put her to work. He'd have her pulling weeds and . . . What do you mean, 'if she stayed'? Are you thinking of staying?"

"No," says Squid, with utter scorn. "I'd go nuts if I had to live here again."

"Then why worry about it?"

"Well, look," says Squid.

Hannah turns back. Murray is rowing slowly along. The water is so calm in the channel, so dazzled by sun, that the clouds are reflected on the surface. It makes it look as though Murray is rowing through the sky, driving the boat toward an ethereal land that floats in the clouds. Tatiana has moved to the stern, trailing her hands in the water. She looks like a very young Alastair.

"She won't want to leave," says Squid.

Let her stay then. Again the thought comes, and again Hannah pushes it from her mind. Squid's not the only one who'd go nuts if she had to live on the island forever.

"I think I'll go have a sleep," says Squid.

"I thought you'd help me with the weathers," Hannah says.

"You don't need any help."

"But I'd like it. You spend all your time in the little house. What do you do in there?"

"Nothing," says Squid.

"Then come and help me. Please? I want to talk to you."

"About what?"

"About you. About Tat."

⁓

They're both amazed by the way the barometer is falling. They compare their readings to the ones Murray recorded three hours before in his small, precise writing. It's plummeting, and the wind is backing into the south.

"It's going to blow," says Hannah.

Squid shrugs. "But not for long."

They settle down at the bench, the radio on. Green Island is just starting; they've got only moments to wait.

Hannah says, "What happened to Erik?"

"Who?" asks Squid.

"Erik," she says. "Erik with a k."

Squid frowns. "Huh?"

Hannah picks up the handset. She whispers across it. "Tatiana's father."

"Ohhhh!" says Squid, wide-eyed. "Well, he died, Mom."

It's Hannah's turn for the weathers. She reads out the data, chats for a moment, and replaces the receiver. Then, remembering the last time, she turns off the volume on the ALAN circuit.

"Yeah, he died," says Squid.

"What happened?"

Squid sighs. She picks up the pencil and draws quick little circles on the top of the desk. "I don't know really. I'm just sure that he's dead. I think I saw it in the paper."

"Really?"

"Look, Mom." It's clear to Hannah from the sound of her voice that this will be the last word on the subject. "That was long ago, okay? And it's over now."

But Hannah can't leave it alone. She would like to, but can't. Again, she sees him, the Viking in his swan-necked boat, his tent with the fluttering flags. She gets up from her chair and hangs the clipboard on its nail. She says, "What was his last name, Squid?"

"I don't remember."

"Oh, come on."

"Johnson. Jensen. I don't know." She jabs at the desk with the pencil. "What difference does it make?"

"Well," says Hannah. She stands behind Squid, looking down at the top of her head. "One day, and one day soon, Tatiana's going to ask you about him. And what will you say then? 'Oh, I don't remember his name'? 'Oh, he looked like a Viking'? Is that what you'll tell her?"

"What else *can* I tell her?" snaps Squid. "I did something incredibly stupid one night, and a million times I've wished I hadn't done it."

"Don't wish that," says Hannah, softly. Her hands close on the back of the chair, not daring to touch her daughter. "Imagine if I wished that *you'd* never been born."

"Oh, you don't understand. You don't know what happened that night."

"Then tell me," says Hannah.

"I *should*." Squid looks up, over her shoulder. "I should tell you what really went on."

There's a fire in her eyes, but Hannah feels only a coldness inside. It's welling up, spreading through her stomach to her spine. Let it go, she tells herself; you don't want to know what *really went on.* Her hands start to tremble. The coldness reaches her fingers.

"Do you want me to?" asks Squid. Her smile is quick, unpleasant. "I will if you want."

"I don't know," says Hannah. All her breath goes out of her. "No. I think you'd better not."

Squid smiles. She *smirks*, with an ugly satisfaction. "I knew you wouldn't," she says. Then she leans forward and comes to her feet, slipping out past the chair. "Can we go now?"

"Yes," says Hannah, sighing. But even now she can't leave it alone. "Just tell me," she says. "Did he hurt you? Tell me that much."

"No, Mom," says Squid. "He didn't mean to hurt me. *Now* can we go?"

⌒

Below the bridge, seagulls sit on a darkening sea, nervously bobbing their heads. The wind is warm but the day much cooler, the sunshine turned to shade. Squid hugs herself in her summery dress. Her arms look chilled and goose-bumped.

Yellow leaves scatter from the alders, drifting down across the path. Hannah's surprised to see so many, surprised *not* to see Murray sweeping them up. Just a year ago his leaf collecting was a full-time job.

She strays to the edge of the path and, boldly, straight onto the grass.

"Mom!" says Squid.

"Oh, it's all right," says Hannah. "Your father won't know."

Squid comes along with her, close to the edge of the cliff. The rocks here are scraped to a whiteness where Murray has whacked them with the lawn mower blades. Squid walks on the outside, nearer the brink, but she keeps looking back, as though she's expecting Murray to pop up from nowhere.

"It's not like you to worry," says Hannah.

"Huh?"

"About something like grass."

"Oh, I wasn't thinking of *that*," says Squid. "It's just weird, not having Tatiana around every minute."

"Sorry," says Hannah. "I should have realized."

"Why? You never thought about that with Alastair and me. We were always alone."

Hannah's not sure if she's meant to feel ashamed, but she doesn't think so. As far as Squid is concerned, whatever was said in the tower will already be forgotten.

"Your father was right about that, at least," says Hannah. "It was one of the best things about the island. As long as you had a bit of common sense you were safe. You weren't about to wander into traffic, or get lured into crime."

"Lured into crime," Squid echoes, though without her usual scorn. "You must have got that from Dad."

"I guess I did." Hannah laughs. They pass the concrete steps and the patch of trampled lawn. The route Hannah has chosen takes them in a curve nearly to the forest.

"I have to watch Tat every second," says Squid.

"Maybe Australia will be different."

"Why? We're not going to be in the *outback*, Mom. We'll be right in the city, in the hugest city there."

"Poor Tat," says Hannah, surprised to find how much she means it. And once more she thinks of Squid staying on the island, though she won't mention *that* again. Squid's anger still stings her. But then, for the first time, she thinks of Tatiana staying behind, of Squid going off and little Tat remaining. The child could spend a year on the island. Maybe the three years until Murray turns sixty-five. He would have his family back and Squid would have her really neat guy. But what about her? Hannah thinks of the winters then, of the storms and the rain, the darkness and cold. And she knows she can't face it. Even the thought is a horror.

"Lured into crime," says Squid again. "I'd kill myself if that happened to Tat."

They circle round by the edge of the trees and meet the boardwalk. But Squid will go no farther. "I really don't want to walk back to the beach," she says. "I'm cold, and I want to get inside."

"Okay," says Hannah. "Whatever you think is best."

chapter thirteen

SQUID OPENS THE FLOORBOARDS AND TOUCHES the books. She takes one from the back of the row, the last—or next to last—of all the ones he filled.

She carries it to the seat in the window, looking out over the forest. At one time it was his sanctuary, and he would sit with a handful of bread crumbs, tempting the sparrows first to the sill and then into the room. In one of the books she has seen little bird footprints covering the pages.

August 27. *Sometimes I wish I was more like Squid. Things are so easy for her. She wants to go look for shells. She wants to search for feathers. For pretty stones and bits of moss. And then she spends hours and hours gluing them together, sanding the shells, wetting the stones with her tongue to see how the colors shine. For her the days go by one after the other, and she has no thought for tomorrow.*

There are things I want to tell her, but she doesn't like talking about stuff she has to think about.

August 28. *Humpbacks. Two of them, the second time they've been here this year. I took the kayak out and played the flute for them. I think they have some understanding that I'm trying to communicate. But it's a tough road ahead.*

August 29. *I went to Dad and told him again that I'd like to study the whales. He couldn't see at first that it means I'll have to go somewhere to do it. And then he took me for a walk. He said that since I was leaving he had something he wanted to show me. We went to the toolshed and he picked up a rake handle. Not the rake but just the handle. Then he took me down the boardwalk and into the forest.*

We talked on the way and he asked when I wanted to go. I said, "Well, as soon as I can." He laughed. "Tomorrow?" he said. I said, "I guess when I finish the high school courses."

We went up through the forest, right to the top of the island, to a tree where the eagles have an aerie. He said, "Alastair, this is where I want to be buried."

He poked his rake handle into the ground and pushed down on the end. It went in easily, four feet or more. "You see," he said. "It's good dirt. It's loam down there. Now, I don't want a stone," he said. "Not even a cross. And for God's sake don't give me a coffin." I said, "Dad, why are you telling me this?" He said he tried to tell Mom, but she didn't understand. She wouldn't go to the place, she said, and walk on his grave. "I just want someone to know," he said. "I've set down directions, but I wanted someone to see where it is."

He made me sit down on the ground. It was covered with bead ruby plants, like water lilies on the land. He said, "Alastair, will you make me a promise?" I said I would try. "Just wait a few more years," he said. "Wait until you're twenty-one before you go away. The years will pass like the blink of an eye, and you'll be old enough then not to have your head turned by the temptations of the world." Then he asked again if I would promise him that.

I did. I had to. In that place, knowing all it meant to him, I had no choice but to promise.

"Alastair," he said, "you're a man of your word and I'll take that as gospel."

I can understand what he wants. If I become the new keeper he won't have to leave when he turns sixty-five. He can stay on the island as long as he wants, or as long as he lives, and that's pretty much the same thing.

But now I feel like a man on Alcatraz. Sentenced to life on the rock.

September 1. The Sikorsky came, bearing technicians. It brought out the mail and a little box for Dad. He gave me the box. He said, "It's a hydrophone, son. If you want to study the whales, I'll help as much as I can."

It's fantastic! I took it out this evening and I really heard for the first time the sounds the humpbacks make. In a way it was disappointing. There were a lot of groans and shouting sounds, here and there a squeal, but none of the songs that they sing. I think maybe they might sing at night.

She remembers that morning, the excitement of the helicopter. And then the disappointment. For the first time in her life a present came for Alastair without one for her.

He opened the box and took out the cables and all the

pieces, and his face lit up with a joy that she hadn't seen in months. He clamped on the headphones and grinned like a lunatic.

"What is that?" she asked.

"A hydrophone," said Alastair. "You can listen under-water."

She said, "Why don't you just go and stick your head underneath?"

It was meant to be funny, or mostly funny. But Alastair was angry. He whistled through his nose. "Can't you at least *pretend* to show interest?" he asked. "This is impor-tant to me."

"Talking to whales?"

"Yes," he said.

"Okay, Dr. Dolittle."

"Oh, grow up," he said.

But she was proud that she'd thought of that name. She taunted him with it for days. And then the fun went out of her game, because Alastair was never there.

September 7. *I think I'm making progress. The sounds, I've decided, aren't meant to be words. They're pictures. They're whole ideas carried in a few different notes. And I think the whales are maybe trying to teach me.*

September 12. *I heard a song! It was wonderful, so long and complex. It was an incredible thing. And in the middle of it, I SAW a picture. I actually saw it. I saw one little verse of the song. An iceberg, from the bottom up, a mass of fish below it, swim-ming in a warm yellow light in front of a wonderful curtain of blue.*

I'm camping on Almost Nothing Atoll. I can't be around people right now.

The pages are wrinkled from water that's soaked them and dried. The writing gets wilder, the letters bigger, and it breaks into verse that goes on for page after page.

> *in a crash of sound*
> *through water rich with sun*
> *i thrust myself up*
> *to the air*
> *to the sky*
> *to another world of quiet and eye-burning bright*
> *to the world of the birds*
> *and i fly*
>
> *my flippers are wings*
> *albatross wings*
> *and i float in this world of above*
> *then tumbling down*
> *i shatter the water*
> *into millions of bubbles*
> *each a part of the sky*

Squid flips through the pages; the verses have no interest for her. She feels a sense that he's close as she reads through weeks that she barely remembers.

September 20. *Another dreary day. Constant rain for three weeks now at least. I try to talk to Dad and he brushes me* *away. He won't listen. "Stop whining," he tells me. CAN'T SOMEBODY HELP???*

September 24. *Raining again. And stormy now too. It's frightening to go out in the kayak, but I make myself do it. Dad's so stubborn that we go on with the chores, and we're all soaking wet before noon. I get sad. Just deeply, terribly sad.*

She would look up, and he would be crying. He would be sitting perfectly still, just staring at nothing, and tears would be going down his cheeks in huge, trembling drops. They would fall from his chin and drop onto his shirt. And she would watch him and think: He doesn't even know it.

"Alastair," she said. "What's the matter?"

"Hmm?" he said. "Oh, nothing. Nothing's the matter."

"You're crying."

He reached up and touched his cheeks. Then he held his fingers up to his glasses, nearly touching the lenses. He squinted through those bottles at the water on his fingers.

"Can't you tell me?" she said.

"Please, Squid," he said. "I just want to think."

September 27. *Four days without a break in the gales. They come one after the other. I can see why men go mad in places like this. I keep thinking of the hanged keeper. His poor ghost trapped on the island. Is that what happens when you die? Will none of us EVER get away?*

At the end of the month, after thirty-four days, came sunshine. It broke through the clouds on the last Sunday morning, as the four of them, all in a row, went across the lawn with tablespoons, digging up the old and flattened dandelions that Murray waged his war against.

It made a patch of light on the grass, and it caught them in their boots and their rain gear as though in a spotlight. Then, one by one, they bent themselves straight and looked up at the break in the clouds. And Squid did a dance. She did a scarecrow dance, twirling herself over the lawn, stumble-dancing past Murray and Hannah, past Alastair, and back down the row again. She laughed and she sang, and she danced in her bright, plastic suit. Then Hannah danced too, and they spun around holding hands. And even Murray joined in, hopping up on one foot, as awkward as a whirligig man.

But Alastair wouldn't dance. He goggled at her through his rain-speckled glasses and stood like a post on the lawn. And Squid teased him for that. She called him names: Mr. Stick-in-the-mud; Alice-the-maid. "Dance, Dr. Dolittle!" she said. And he smiled.

It was the smallest, saddest smile she'd ever seen. His face cracked with it, like a window hit with a stone. It was hardly a smile at all.

But it was there.

The next day was a bit brighter, and the one after that even more so. Then the sky was bigger and bluer than ever before. And all of them but Alastair forgot that it had rained for more than a month.

Alastair was like the droplets on the lawn. He vanished with the sun.

"I think he's changed," said Squid. "He's just not the same anymore."

She ate breakfast at the big house; it was too lonely at Gomorrah.

"Does he talk about it?" asked Hannah.

"He doesn't talk," she said.

Hannah buttered Murray's toast as he worked his way through his oatmeal. "What can we do?" she asked.

"The best thing?" said Squid. "Send him to town. When the boat comes, let him go into town for a week."

Murray glanced up. "And I suppose you'd go with him?"

"Well, he can't go alone." She grinned.

"And he can't go at all," said Murray. "All his life I've taught him to face up to his problems. You take trouble head-on, not with your back to it." He asked for jam with his toast. "Yet here, all of a sudden, at the first sign of a problem—"

"The first sign!" said Hannah. "Oh, Murray. Look around you!"

"At what?" he asked, bewildered.

"He's miserable here."

Squid turned to her mother. "You know what it is?" she said. "Dad's frightened that Alastair won't come home."

Murray's eyes blazed. "Is that so?" he said. "Well, I'll have you know he's given me his word. He won't be leaving until he turns twenty-one."

Hannah's hand stopped in midair, a smear of jam like

blood on the blade of her knife. "When did he say that?" she asked.

"Not long ago."

"Why?"

"Why not!" snapped Murray.

Hannah backed down; she wouldn't argue with Murray. She put the jam on his bread and—it might have been to herself—said, "I didn't know that's how he thought."

"Och, it's a paradise here, if you'll only open your eyes to see it." Murray took the toast. It was cold and hard, and it crunched as he bit it. "The boy's got more than enough to keep himself busy as long as he lives."

<hr />

Squid left the table with her breakfast half finished. She went down to the beach and launched the glass-bottomed boat. She rowed through the lagoon, out to the channel with the sun blinding back from the glass. The bow was aimed for Almost Nothing Atoll, and her arms, like machines, pumped the oars around and around.

Water burbled up behind her and rippled down the sides. When the boat skittered sideways she brought it straight with the oars. Then she slid them inside when she was close to the island, and the boat slewed around with its stern to the shore. A huge cloud of birds rose from the trees; they circled around her, ravens and gulls.

It was the sun in his glasses; that was all she saw at first. He stood absolutely still, peering down at her between the cedar boughs. His arms were spread across them, and he looked as wild and wary as an otter, ready to flee—to slither away—if she came any nearer.

Squid stood up in the boat. Her feet straddled the pane of glass; her hands were on her hips. "You told Dad you were staying until you're twenty-one," she said.

He didn't move. He came no closer.

"Alastair," she said. "You tell me if it's true."

The boughs shook as he lowered his arms. They swept in from the sides, closing around him.

"Are you going to be like this until you're twenty-one?" She shouted at the trees. "You'll be a crazy old loon by then. They'll have to take you off in a strait-jacket."

There was no answer.

"Alastair," she said. "Alastair!"

She plopped herself down on the seat. She fitted the oars into the rowlocks. And Alastair came out from the trees.

He came slowly; he stumbled on a root. He wore gray sweatpants without any shirt, and his stomach was round and white. He stepped down from rock to rock—he was barefoot, she saw—and sat by the edge of the water. He said, "Did you come out here just to ask me that?"

"Yes," she said. "I thought you had plans. You were going off to college. You were going to *do* something."

He paddled a foot in the water. He looked up at her, then down. "Dad needs me here," he said.

"He doesn't."

Alastair shrugged. "Well, I've told him I'm staying. I have to make the best of it now."

She stared at him: at his hunched shoulders with the bones sticking out; his thin twigs of arms; his funny, impossible hair; his glasses; and the thin cords of white rope that dangled from his waistband, cinching tight the pants that were too baggy to fit. "And this is it?" she asked. "This is you doing your *best?*"

On the fifteenth day of October, a kayaker arrived at Lizzie. He was tall and bronze, like a statue loosed from a pedestal. He landed on the strip of white sand where Squid was gathering shells.

She carried them in her skirt, holding it up high at the front to make a sling for the little clams and the periwinkles. She turned around and he was there, the tallest man she had ever seen.

There was only a breath of wind, and it blew from her back. It pressed her skirt between her legs and ruffled through her hair. The man looked down at her, smiling. She said, "What are you looking at?"

He told her, "I didn't think mermaids were real."

They sat on the beach, up high by the logs where the sun made white heat from the sand. The kayaking man stretched flat on his back. He opened and closed his legs; he swept his arms as far as he could reach. He made an angel in the sand.

Squid was thirteen. She had never before sat on the beach with a man who made angels. She showed him the shells, though it seemed awfully silly, because he wanted her to. He took each one from her fingers, so that their hands were always touching, and after he'd looked at the swirls on the white—all colors of swirls—he put them down in a pattern. It was the most beautiful thing in the world, a spiral of shells. And when she stood up, she saw that it was one big shell that he'd made from them all.

They went for a walk on the beach, close to the water, and the waves came up and covered her toes. They sucked at her feet, and now and then he had to reach out to hold her.

Alastair was at the end of the sand. He rose up from the space behind the logs; he stepped ungainly across them. He looked half as tall as the kayaking man, very white and small beside him, as crazy as old Ben Gunn. His face was twisted into a look of dismay, and his eyes—unnaturally big in the glasses—blinked very quickly. "I'm Alastair," he said, his eyes going like strobes. "Who are you?"

chapter fourteen

*H*ANNAH MAKES HER WAY DOWN THE boardwalk. Only the tops of the trees feel the wind, and a thin shower of needles falls at her feet. They're brown and ocher, covering the planks. She can hear the needles falling as they slither through the leaves.

She's nearly at the meadow when Murray's voice booms out, up ahead, "Ready or not!" and Tatiana's little feet patter along the boardwalk.

There's a flash of crimson clothes, and Tatiana bursts around the corner far ahead. She's running in her clumsy way, looking back, watching for Murray behind her.

"Here I come," shouts Murray, and Tatiana leaps from the boardwalk, into the huckleberries and the broad green leaves of the skunk cabbage.

Hannah smiles. The game was always a favorite, with Squid most of all, though not so much with Alastair. He was good at the hiding, but hopeless at the seeking.

The boardwalk shakes as Murray comes running. "You better be hiding!" he shouts.

She can hear Tatiana: a rustle of leaves; a giggle. With her eyes, she follows the sound. And she gasps.

It's the shoes that startle Hannah.

~

Squid was found right here, just yards from where Tatiana huddles in the moss. It was Alastair who found her, on that cold morning too late for autumn and too early for winter.

He came running to the big house. He came all winded, scratched on his face by branches and thorns.

"It's Squid," he said. "It's Squid, and she's dying."

Hannah was putting up jars of huckleberry jam. The one in her hand fell to the floor, smashing into a pool of red juice and shining glass, splattering the counters and the walls. She raced from the house, and Murray came from the generator shed, sprinting right over the lawn. They followed Alastair back to the forest, back down the boardwalk to this little hollow.

Squid was lying on her side, sprawled on a bed of thick, yellow moss. The vomit that dribbled from her mouth and oozed through the ground was just that same color.

"I saw her shoes," said Alastair. "I was on the boardwalk. It was all I could see, the red of her shoes."

They were a shocking color, a lurid crimson brighter than anything natural. They looked obscene, splayed out on the moss.

Murray jumped down from the boardwalk. He grabbed Squid's shoulders and rolled her over, onto her back. Her head flopped sideways, her tongue poking out past her lips, her eyes—not quite closed—showing moons of white. Murray put his cheek to her mouth, his fingers to her neck. "She's breathing," he said. "Her pulse is slow, but she's breathing."

Underneath her were little bundles—leaves and mushrooms and roots—bound with strands of orange and lavender wool. Hannah recognized some, but not all. There were things in those bundles that Squid had been taught never to touch.

Murray said, "She's been eating this stuff?"

Alastair saw the pattern; Alastair had studied the plants. "They're abortifacients," he said. Then, "Oh, Jiminy, Dad! She's pregnant."

Murray didn't even flinch. "Let's hope she still is."

He carried her up to the house, to the big house and not Gomorrah. Her hands and her feet flopped down, swinging as he carried her.

⌒

"Where, oh where can you be?" chants Murray now, appearing round a bend in the boardwalk. He stops there, looking into the forest. "I'm getting closer, Tatiana. Is that a wee person I can see?"

Tatiana giggles, and Murray turns toward the sound. "Oh, Hannah!" he says. And he blushes.

Hannah stares at him as he comes up to her side. She shows him with a tilt of her head where Tatiana has hidden herself. "Come out of there, Tat," she says.

There's a look of disappointment on the child's face, her little game destroyed. Slowly, she stands up.

"Do you see where she's come to?" asks Hannah.

It dawns slowly on Murray. Then he says, "The child couldn't know. You didn't have to spoil her fun, Hannah."

"Well, I'm certainly sorry."

Murray frowns. "Och, what's the matter?" he asks.

She can't explain. The island has cold spots of horror. There are some she won't visit and others she seeks, from time to time, for a strange pleasure in the melancholy that they give her. The meadow is one of the worst, and it doesn't seem proper to have it used for a game, to fill it with laughter and shouting.

"I came to find you," she says. "You were gone for so long, but I see you're all right."

"We're fine," says Murray. "Playing hide-and-seek." He turns to Tatiana. "Come on, Tatty. We'll both have to find a hiding place now. It looks like your grandma is it."

Murray can be infectious, spreading pleasure like germs. Hannah, reluctant at first, joins in the game. She stands with her hands on her eyes, counting slowly to a hundred. Then, "Here I come!" she shouts. And now she's running, feeling the wind, seeing the bushes blur past, and she's laughing.

⌒

The sky is dark with clouds when Hannah comes out from the forest, a step ahead of Murray. Bands of purple and black rolling high above the island. She watches them, and is halfway to the big house before she sees that Squid is there, sitting on the steps, looking lonely and forgotten.

For a moment, Hannah feels pity for her daughter. But she sees that Squid has raided Murray's treasured stock of cider and sits with a bottle in one hand, a cigarette in the other.

"We've had great fun," says Murray, trudging toward her with Tatiana at his side. The gravel crunches under his feet. "You missed a fine game of hide-and-go-seek."

"I could hear you," says Squid. "You're happy here, aren't you, Tat?"

Tatiana nods vigorously. Her red clothes, her sweet grin, make her look like an elf.

Squid smokes, then drinks. She holds up the bottle. "You don't mind, do you, Dad?"

"Not at all." Nothing can spoil his mood.

"Tat, you go play," says Squid. "Go and look at Old Glory, okay?"

Tatiana presses herself against Murray. She tugs on his trousers, gazing up. "Play me sandbox?" she asks.

Murray is absolutely thrilled.

"No," says Squid. She empties her bottle and drops the cigarette inside. She swirls it around, and smoke comes up through the mouth. "Dad, I've got to talk to you."

Hannah nearly gasps. Squid is standing up, putting her bottle down on the steps, on a little round stain that it has left on the wood.

"Can't it wait?" asks Murray.

Squid shakes her head. "Go on, Tatiana. Go and look at Old Glory or something while I talk to your grandpa."

It seems she means to tell Murray right now that she's leaving as soon as she can, in a month at the most, that she's taking little Tat to Australia and won't ever be back to the island.

And Hannah won't let her do that. "Yes, it can wait,"

she says quickly. "It's going to rain very soon, so you two go and play in the sandbox, then we'll all have hot chocolate. We'll all have a talk."

"But, Mom—" says Squid.

"It's fine."

Squid thumps herself back on the steps, her arms crossed. Murray shrugs, then wanders off with Tatiana.

"Mom, why did you stop me?" asks Squid.

"Come inside," says Hannah, starting up the steps.

<hr />

This is where they brought her, through this door as she lay like a sack in Murray's arms, those red shoes dangling. He put her on the sofa, and he looked a hundred years old.

Squid lay unconscious for only an hour, cocooned in a yellow blanket. Then she woke, and she groaned. She threw up in a bucket that Hannah had soaked with ammonia.

"How do you feel?" asked Murray. He hadn't moved from her side. He had wetted her forehead with water and held her hand in his.

"I feel okay," said Squid. "But this ammonia's making me sick."

Alastair, too, had stayed with her, in a chair at the foot of the sofa. He had cried all the time, wringing his hands. But now he smiled, and patted her shoes.

Squid looked up half-dazedly at the faces hovering round her.

"Well, you're back in Kansas now," said Murray.

"What?" she said. Squid had never seen The Wizard of Oz.

"You gave us a fright," he said. "You gave us a terrible scare."

She reached under the blanket, feeling at her stomach, down to her legs.

"There's nothing wrong," said Murray. "You're as whole as whole can be."

She was up on her feet that evening. She went back to Gomorrah, and Murray waited a day before he faced her with his inquisition. He paced as she sat in a chair.

"You're pregnant," he said suddenly. "Or you think you are."

"What do you mean?" she said.

"Now, don't deny it, Squid."

He thought of himself as Perry Mason, or Hercule Poirot, perhaps. A cunning sort of person. He paced back and forth in front of the floor lamp, and his shadow loomed across her.

"You were trying to get rid of a baby," he said. Then, "Didn't you think?" he cried. "You could have killed your-self." He pulled at his hair. "Tell me what you did."

"I gathered the plants," said Squid. "I spent days col-lecting—"

"Och! How did you get a baby?"

She told them about Erik. It was the first they'd heard of him. She described his kayak with its elegant prow, his tent and the flags on the poles. She said, "Alastair met him. Alastair saw us together."

"And where's Alastair?" asked Murray.

"I don't know!" she said.

Hannah leads her daughter through to the kitchen. She gets the milk from the fridge, a pan from the cupboard. Murray's as fussy about hot chocolate as he is about anything. It has to be made the old-fashioned way, from cocoa powder and sugar, with the tiniest bit of ground coffee.

Squid doesn't offer to help. She leans on the counter, looking out through the window toward Murray's sandbox.

Hannah puts the pan on the stove and sees that her hands are shaking.

"Well?" says Squid.

Hannah takes a deep breath. "This isn't right, what you're doing," she says. "You can't just turn around and leave forever."

Squid doesn't answer. A look as dark as the coming storm passes over her face. From outside comes Tat's shrill voice, laughing with excitement.

"It isn't fair," says Hannah. "What about Tatiana?"

"Oh, you don't care about Tat. You're just thinking of Dad," says Squid. "And yourself. You just want what *you* want."

"That isn't true. You don't even know what I want." Hannah pours milk into the pan, letting it slosh up the sides. "Can't you see the difference in your own daughter? Can't you see how happy she is?"

"So was Alastair once."

"For heaven's sake, Squid. I'm not asking you to keep her here for *fourteen years*." Hannah is nearly shouting, nearly crying. "Just a month, that's all. The month you promised." She turns on the burner and stirs the milk with a wooden spoon. "And then you can decide what's next."

"I already know what's next. We've got visas and tickets—"

"Then what harm will it do to stay for a month?"

Squid stares out the window, blinking quickly. She touches her eyes with her fingers. "What happened to the men against the girls?" she asks.

Hannah can't keep from smiling. "No one's ganging up on you, Squid. Your father doesn't know what I'm telling you."

Squid sobs. "Well, neither do I."

Hannah leaves the stove and holds her daughter. She holds her as hard as she can, and then Squid's arms wrap round her waist, and they lean against each other. "I just don't want to lose you again," Hannah says.

They stand like that until the smell of burning milk wafts from the pan and pries them apart. Hannah kisses Squid's forehead, then smiles. She empties the pan and starts all over again.

"I can't stay," says Squid. "Even if I wanted to. I see Dad with Tatiana, and all I can think about is Alastair."

"Alastair loved your dad."

"But he said some awful things about him."

"Like what?"

"Mom, you don't want to know."

"Tell me this, then," says Hannah. "What did the two of you talk about just before he died? What did he say in the small house?"

"The same things he always did." Squid is helping now. She's measuring coffee into the grinder, and the beans are ticking against the metal. "He talked about leaving the island. How Dad—and you—wouldn't let him."

Hannah stirs the milk, staring at the swirls that follow her wooden spoon round and round the pan. "Did he tell you he was going to kill himself?" And the effort it takes to ask that question leaves her nearly breathless.

"No, Mom," says Squid. "That's the only thing he never told me."

The storm comes with a quick, heavy shower of rain. Huge drops splash across the lawn. The wind sock stiffens, and turns. The clouds close in, walling the island with darkness.

Through the evening the lightkeeper's family sits in the front room of the big house, hearing the sea and the wind. The bell rings once, and then twice, and rain slams on the roof, gushing through the pipes and into the cistern with an eerie wail. But the eaves still overflow, cascading past the window. The lawn is a lake.

Squid says, "I'd forgotten it could be like this."

"Och, it's nothing," says Murray. He's on the sofa with Tat at his side. "Wait for December. The nights so long there's hardly a day between them. Waves like houses. Storms never stopping."

A seagull is carried across the lawn like a windblown umbrella. The surf is louder, bashing at the island. The whirligigs rattle like old bicycles. And Squid lifts her head at the sound.

"Did you know," she asks, "that Alastair was scared of the whirligigs?"

"Och, he wasn't," snorts Murray.

"It's true." Squid nods. "The night the *Cape Caution* sank, Old Glory fell off his pole. And just after the *Odd Fellow* sank, one of the windmilling birds did the same thing. Alastair said it must be an omen. He said if a whirligig falls, a boat is surely doomed."

"Hmm," says Murray. "I didn't know that."

Squid sighs. "I guess he only told me."

"Och, he was a poor soul. Always fretting about somebody else."

The talk brings a gloom to the big house. Murray puts his arm around Tat. Half-asleep, she wriggles down against him. There are the wind and the rain and the gurgle of water, and Squid is close to tears.

"This is awful," she says. "What do you do in the middle of winter? How can you stand it like this?"

"Life goes on," says Murray. "But I'll tell you . . ."

Hannah feels the hairs stir on the back of her neck. She wants to fling out some words, changing the subject.

"It gets pretty lonely sometimes," he says. "With your mother away and all."

So now Squid knows. Hannah can see it in her eyes, the way a slot machine jingles and blinks as the numbers roll round. She can feel her making connections, shaping a picture from the pieces she's learned.

And then she says, in her singsong way, "I didn't know you did that, Mom."

"Oh, yes," says Murray. "I batch it in the winters now." He's not complaining; he even smiles fondly at Hannah. "I suppose you gave your mother a taste for the city life, Squid."

The helicopter came for Squid in April. It came in a hurry, slanted down at the nose, roaring over the island with its belly nearly touching the trees.

That morning, before dawn, Hannah had been jolted from a nightmare by the sound of her daughter screaming. She had heard doors slamming as Squid fled from Gomorrah, then another long shriek from outside. She had hardly thrown off the covers before Squid came flying up the stairs and into the room, holding her stomach, shouting, "My baby!" There was blood in a bright patch on her nightgown, and in smears along her fingers. Murray, in blue pajamas, had dashed off to the radio.

They were waiting on the pad when the helicopter came. Hannah believed they would *all* get in, that they would fly together to Rupert, straight to the hospital. Whatever happened to Squid's baby, she thought, it would be the end of Lizzie. They would find a house on a hill, looking east to the mountains, and none of them would ever come back to the island. Murray would attend to their things.

But only the girls went away. They flew to a world that Squid barely knew. Hannah found a room and Squid had her baby. It was the happiest, most normal baby Hannah had ever seen, and for the first time in a decade she said a prayer of thanksgiving.

Squid started at school, in a special class with other young mothers. She filled her life so full of friends and new things and little Tatiana that there wasn't room for

Hannah. When the baby was three months old, Squid said, "Mom, you should go back to the island."

"Yes," said Hannah.

They were driving each other crazy.

⁓

Squid is sitting in the old rocking chair where Murray held her as a baby. She sits and watches him as he plays with Tatiana, looking neither happy nor sad. Hannah can't imagine what she's thinking. Does she feel at home at all?

The island was never the same for Hannah after that stay in Prince Rupert. She came back in September, just as summer was ending. The house felt like a bunker, herself and Murray sealed inside it. He carried on just as before, reading about the plants and the animals as though he was still catching up to Alastair, but Hannah couldn't bear the silence and the loneliness. By Halloween she was back in Prince Rupert, only to find that Squid had gone south to Vancouver and vanished into the city.

It was heartbreaking. Alastair was gone forever, and it seemed that Squid was too. "She's been lured into crime," said Murray, but Hannah imagined things worse than that. Then the last boat of the year brought a letter from Squid, such a cheery letter that she couldn't have thought anyone had worried about her. She had finished school and found a job that paid nearly as much as Murray earned. After that one, her letters came sporadically, sometimes two or three at once, sometimes none for months at a time. But she never called on the ALAN circuit. And she never asked for anything.

Hannah smiles at her now. What a beautiful girl she is, but still such a child. Slumped in the chair, lazily rocking herself, she seems to have no worries or fears. She has become exactly what Hannah always thought she would: a strong and independent person.

On the sofa, Murray and Tat thread jingle shells on a bit of string. Murray does the threading; Tat only jingles. She's happy with the sound they make.

"Whale," she says.

"No, no." Murray shakes the string of thin white plates. "Jingle shells." And Tat says too: "Jingle shells."

"Good girl," praises Murray.

"Whale."

"Och," he says.

But she's adamant. She stands up on her chair and shouts the word. She points at the window and shouts it again.

Hannah says, "I think she's trying to tell you something."

"Och, I can see that," says Murray. "What I don't understand is what. Or why."

"And there's no use in trying to figure it out," says Squid. She stretches her legs, rocking forward until her heels are on the carpet. "We should have our talk now, Mom."

"Oh, let's leave it for later," says Hannah. Too much has changed now that her secret is out.

"Then I guess I'll go to the small house," says Squid.

Squid is proven right: the storm is hard, but short. By morning it has passed, and the gulls wheel and dip above the lagoon. Something has excited them. Their cries are shrill and piercing.

As though she's been brought back to the schedule of her childhood, Squid comes to the door very early. She has Tatiana with her, and she's ready to leave the girl and go. "I'll just walk down and see what the birds are doing," says Squid. But Murray won't allow it.

"You know the rules," he says. "Work first, play after." Then he looks at Tatiana. "But, och, there's nothing needing doing today."

When they set off for the beach, Murray in the lead, it's hard for Hannah not to linger far behind. Four people, going in pairs, is too much like the old days, as though Tatiana has taken the place of Alastair. They go at her pace, and it's Tat—instead of him—who notices how the cobwebs glisten, how the ferns droop sodden leaves. It's a long, nostalgic walk for Hannah. And at the end, at the beach, they gather in a quiet knot where the boardwalk leaves the forest. They can only gawk at what they see.

The whale, the humpback, is stranded in the sand.

It's enormous, and more than that. There's not a word to say how huge it is. Twice as high as Murray, longer than the big house, it's stretched along the height of beach with its head nearly touching the logs. The flukes lie flat, the flippers spread like scalloped wings. In the massive head the eye seems tiny. It swivels round toward them.

Murray is the first to run across the beach. Crows and ravens rise from the whale like hordes of flies. The gulls circle, and the air is filled with a scream and a clamor of birds.

Squid holds Tat in place. The child is staring down the

beach; already she's in tears. "Oh, Tat," says Hannah. She feels the same; she feels just the same as that.

She steps to the sand. Along the beach is a line of kelp and wood and small, dead crabs. It's a ragged, jumbled line where sand fleas hop through steaming piles of green and brown. It marks the reach of the sea at the storm's high tide, and it crosses under the whale far behind its flippers. Half the humpback's length lies on a part of the beach that was never touched by the sea. It drove itself ashore; it almost crawled toward the trees.

But, incredibly, Murray stands at the nose and tries to push it back. He digs in his feet and puts his shoulder to the whale, to a knob of leathery skin. He looks so tiny there, so helpless. And soon he gives it up.

"Why?" he says. "Hannah, why?"

She has no answer. She holds her hand against the whale and in her fingers and her palm she feels a tremor deep inside it. The whale is breathing, but not with spouts and tremendous blasts of air. The skin at the blowholes flutters like the lips of a snoring man. The breaths are long, and faint, and weak. All its weight is resting on its lungs.

Hannah rubs her hand in circles. He—surely it's a he—feels cold to her. Along the edges of the flippers grow barnacles the size of her fist. His mouth is long, curving at the end. Above it, on the sloping jaw, are lovely sculpted grooves. And higher still, the dark, round eye is open. The pupil turns toward her. She can see a knowledge in it, a resignation of its death.

The flipper ripples on the sand. And from inside the

whale comes a long and dreadful groan. The eye pivots away.

Tatiana is coming. Squid has to hurry to keep up, her hand on the child's collar.

"Let her go," shouts Hannah. "Let her go."

"It will crush her!" says Squid.

"No. He won't do that."

And Squid hangs back as Tatiana races splay-legged up the beach in a rattle of her jingle shells.

She throws herself at the whale. She hits it full length, with a sickly thud, like the sound of bread dough punched by a fist. She spreads her arms and tries to hug it, this vast, enormous thing. The flipper moves again, scraping up the sand. The huge flukes rise and, sagging, fall in place.

And Murray asks, sadly, "Why?"

"I don't know," says Hannah. "Who could answer that?"

"Alastair could," says Squid. She stands with her hands in the pockets of her jeans, her legs crossed in a clumsy way. "They don't want to drown." She shrugs. "That's what he said. It scares them to think of drowning."

Murray walks away from the whale. He steps back to the logs. "How do you know this?" he asks.

"We talked about it. It's what he wrote in his book." She glances up the height of the whale, her head tipping back. "He wrote down what they were saying. He wrote down their songs in his book."

Murray's too sad to be angry. But he has to raise his voice to be heard at all. The birds are screaming more loudly as the whale is slowly dying. "Are you reading this book?" he says.

"He gave it to me once." Squid uncrosses her legs and kneels in the sand. "He asked me to read it, to see what I thought. He asked me if he was going crazy."

"Where is it?" asks Murray. "No. Fetch it here. Squid, run and fetch it."

chapter fifteen

O ctober 3. *They're back! I turned on the hydrophone, sure there would be nothing but static again, but heard the humpbacks instead. I don't know where they've been, and I'm pretty sure they'll be leaving for the winter in a couple of weeks or so. There's something in the song that sounds like goodbye. I think I understand them now, and I want to go with them. I want to be with them always.*

I sat on Almost Nothing Atoll this afternoon and read everything I've written. Either I'm right or I'm not, I don't know which. But if I'm not I must be crazy.

October 5. *I tried to talk to Dad again, but he thinks what I'm doing is nonsense. He said, "Let's assume you're right, and whales have a language. What makes you think you could understand it? If you heard a lot of Chinamen talking, would you know what they were saying?"*

Maybe he's right. But I think I deserve a chance to find out. I told him—AGAIN—I need computers and spectrographs. He said, "Alastair, everything you need is under your nose. It's in your books, boy. Go back to your books." I told him it's NOT in the books. No one has ever listened the way that I have.

October 6. *The work never stops. I do my chores and then go off by myself. I don't know how long I can last.*

I'm drowning. Can't breathe, can't surface, can't escape. Dad just WILL NOT LISTEN!!!! Mom can't persuade him and won't even try anymore. Thank God for Squid. It would be HELL here if it wasn't for Squid. I'm afraid to tell her that I think I'm falling in love.

Squid looks up from the book. So that was it, the thing that has haunted her for so long. Alastair was in love with her.

She shakes her head. "That's *it?*" she asks herself. "*That's* the terrible thing?" She nearly laughs, until an image of him comes into her mind, so serious and worried, sunlight making his glasses white and his eyes invisible. Why was he afraid to tell her that?

She's horrible to me sometimes. If she hated me she couldn't act much worse. But she's the only one who cares, and I can see it every time she looks at me. I think she's maybe in love with me too, but doesn't want me to know it, and that's why she acts mean. I think she would like us to go away together.

She looks at the book, and past it. The floorboards are open, the mat pulled askew. She looks at his desk, at his table, at his funny and slanted shelves. They're all full of Alastair's treasures; everything he owned is here.

The useless book holder that she made him is high on the opposite wall. The dozens of necklaces that she tied with her shells are heaped inside a wooden box printed with Japanese characters, itself a salvage from the beach. His favorite shirt is folded on the back of a chair; his shoes, side by side, are underneath. On the dresser is his flute. It's as though he never left or, having left, now comes home to Gomorrah.

Why was he frightened to tell her that he loved her? Did he think she would only mock him?

Mr. *Stick-in-the-mud*. She hears her voice; she sees herself dancing around him. *You're nuts; you're crazy as a bug.*

He was right: She couldn't have acted any worse. She never listened to the things he told her.

Squid sighs, then flips forward through the pages.

October 15. *There was a guy on the beach today. I saw Squid with him and felt all sick inside. Squid didn't want me around. She said, "Why don't you go and talk to the whales?" They laughed as I walked away. Squid said, "It's true. My brother talks to the whales." It's a funny thing. The guy looks a bit like me. Maybe that's why Squid likes him so much.*

He looked nothing like Alastair. He was tall and tanned, with eyes like bits of sunlit sea. He was older than her by ten years or more, and he made her feel grown up; he made her feel beautiful.

He asked her name, and when she told him Squid, he laughed and said no, that couldn't be right. "It's Elizabeth," she told him, then, blushing. But he said even that wasn't pretty enough. He said, "I'll call you Sabrina—Neptune's daughter."

He made a spear from a stick, then waded out and caught a crab. It was a little red rock crab, and it squirmed on the point of the spear as he held it up. He grinned and grunted, a Viking's cry.

Over a crackling fire he cooked the crab. He served it to her on a clamshell, then wiped the juices that dribbled on her chin. When the sun went down, they lay in the sand and stared at the stars. He took her hand to lead her into his tent.

She stayed with him until it was nearly dawn. And then, barefoot—with her shoes in her hand—she ran up through the forest and along the boardwalk. At the center of the island, near the dark banks of the middens, Alastair was waiting. He grabbed her arm as she passed a stump, and she nearly screamed from the fright she got.

He looked wild, like a hermit of the woods. "Get lost," she said, and shook his arm away.

He grabbed her again. "You stayed all night," he said.

"So what?"

"You kissed him."

"So *what?*" she said again. And then, like a child, "You spied on me!"

"What else did you do?"

She pulled away a second time, surprised by the strength in Alastair's arms. She marched along the boardwalk, but he hurried past and blocked her way.

"Come on," he said. "What did you do?"

"It's none of your *business*," she said. "You stupid freak; why were you watching?"

"Are you leaving with him?" His face was only inches from hers, his glasses gleaming like owls' eyes in the dawn. "Are you? Is he taking you away?"

"Maybe," she said, just to taunt him.

"Squid!" he shouted. And then he collapsed. He fell down at her feet, crying with heartbroken sobs.

She was too angry to comfort him, to tell him she *wasn't* going away. Erik would be leaving by himself as soon as the tide came in. She had told him, "I'll come and say good-bye," but he hadn't wanted that; he didn't like to say goodbyes.

"You can't leave," said Alastair, sobbing. "You just can't."

"I can do whatever I want," she told him.

"Oh, Squid," he said. "Please." He held on to her ankles. His forehead touched the top of her foot. "You don't even know him. He was just telling you things. Whatever he thought you would like. He's just a jerk, Squid. He's just a stupid jerk." He sniffed and cried. "And Sabrina *wasn't* Neptune's daughter."

She laughed then. She knelt down and put an arm on her brother's shoulders. She could feel his bones shaking. "Hey, quit it," she said, softly.

"Do you love him?" he asked.

"Maybe," she said. "I guess so."

"Do you love him more than me?"

"Oh, Alastair," she said.

"Do you?"

He still wouldn't look at her. He huddled on the

boardwalk, in the gray of the new morning, with his hands drawn in to cover his face. His glasses had fallen onto the planks.

"Oh, Alastair," she said again, but tenderly now. "I'd do anything for you. I'd do *anything* to make you happy." She hugged him with all her strength. "Anything."

October 17. *The natives are getting restless.*

The book is empty after that. It's the last thing that Alastair wrote. In little more than a month, he was dead.

Squid closes the floorboards. She drags the mat into place. She tucks the book under her arm and tramps down the stairs. On the lawn, she walks faster; on the boardwalk, she sprints. She's racing her thoughts, trying to outrun them.

It's the same way she went years ago, a month after Erik left, when Alastair was still alive. She carried plants then, small bundles tied with wool. She remembers the taste of them, the fear of knowing that something was wrong when the forest started leaping and spinning around her, when the sky turned white, then red, and finally black.

And suddenly Murray was mopping her face. Alastair was holding her feet. They were both angry, but Alastair most of all. Late that night, in Gomorrah, he whistled like a steam train through his nostrils as she lay on the sofa with a blanket pulled up to her shoulders.

"What if you'd died?" he said, looking down. "Didn't you think about that?"

"None of that stuff could kill me," she said.

"It almost did."

"But it *didn't*." She kicked the blanket into a wad at her feet. "It didn't even kill the baby."

"How do you know that?" he asked.

She rolled her eyes. "Because nothing came out, of course."

"Oh, Jiminy!" he said. "Squid, you're so stupid."

He took his hydrophone down from the shelf. He pressed the transducer onto her stomach, on top of her blouse, then put on the earphones and squinted with the effort of listening. "I can't hear anything," he said.

"Don't expect it to sing," she told him.

"Shhh!" He moved the transducer back and forth. "I don't think there's anything there. I don't think there *ever* was."

"Well, I can feel it," she said. "Mr. Genius. I can't explain it, but I *know* it's there."

He tossed the hydrophone down in a tangle. He dropped into the chair by the window and looked out at the darkness through his own reflection. A black-headed wren came and stood on the sill, but Alastair didn't even seem to notice it.

Squid stared at him, at the side of his face, and she saw how frightened he was. "Alastair, don't worry," she said. "It's going to work out."

"How?" he asked.

"Erik's coming back. He promised he would. He told me, 'I'll come with the geese.' "

Alastair snorted.

"It's true," she said. "He'll come back and I'll say, 'Look! You're a dad.' And he'll be happy, you see. Nothing will matter to Erik."

The wren hopped down from the sill. Alastair didn't move.

"So what's to worry about?" asked Squid.

"He'll take you away. Won't he?"

"We didn't talk about that," said Squid.

"But he will."

"I don't *know*," she snapped. "Maybe he'll stay on the island and Dad will build us a house. You can go to college, maybe, and when you come back you can be the keeper when Dad retires. Okay? Whatever you want, that's what we'll do."

"Yeah, right," said Alastair.

"Then what *do* you want?" she asked, angered by his gloom.

"Who cares?" he asked. "I'll never get what *I* want. Are you so stupid that you can't see that?"

"Don't call me stupid," she said.

"Stupid, stupid."

"Oh, get out," she said. "Go on, Alastair. Go play with the whales, or whatever you do. I'm sick of looking at you."

He blinked at her, then started to cry, but she didn't take her words back. He got up from his chair, found his coat and his flute, and stood for a moment at the door.

She didn't bother to look at him. "I hope Erik *does* take me away," she said. "I hate being stuck here with you."

It was the last thing she ever said to him. He opened

the door, walked out to the porch, and she never saw him again.

⁓

Murray hasn't moved from the log when Squid arrives, breathless, back at the beach. His elbows on his knees, his head in his hands, he looks the same as he did the day Alastair died. Squid opens the book and hands it to him.

Hannah keeps walking, dragging her fingers on the whale's skin, past the nose and down the side. "He's breathing so hard," she says. "He shudders when he breathes."

The whale is slowly sinking into the beach. He's spreading across it, flattening out. Little Tatiana is huddled right against him, in the curve where the flipper joins the body. It seems almost as though the whale is holding her, and she leans her minuscule weight on the towering wall of the humpback. Her ear and her hands are pressed against the wall of flesh.

"Singing," she says. "Listen, Mom. Singing inside."

Squid puts her ear to the whale. The sound, to her, is only a rumble and a wheeze. It's the beating of a failing heart and the gasp of crushed lungs; the squirting of blood down shriveling veins. It's the sound of dying, and it scares her.

"Singing," says Tat.

"That's right," says Squid. "He's telling a story."

⁓

Murray stands by the head of the whale. He looks like a preacher, the book for a Bible. In a slow voice, deep as the oceans, he reads aloud what Alastair has written.

"From the land I came. On the land
the creator made me.
And there I will return when
one day
I am wearied. And at peace."

chapter sixteen

HANNAH STANDS BEHIND MURRAY. SHE looks over his shoulder, down at the book. The page that he's reading is mottled with seawater stains. In places the letters are smudged by a spatter of drops that might have been spindrift or rain.

She finds it strange to think of her son writing this. He was always so tidy and neat, but the words are a scrawl, as though he'd been furiously setting them down, trying to keep up with the whales.

In effervescence the calves are born
in a phosphorescent sea

Squid is watching Tatiana more closely than she ever has. She doesn't seem happy with the place her daughter has chosen, a crease between the sand and thirty tons of whale. But Tat's peculiar face is free of all worries; it's an expression almost of rapture.

And Murray reads aloud, in a voice that's an echo of Alastair's.

"The Orcas come, the killing whales
burning through the sea
with meteor tails of glowing green
in a blackness without sun.
And I see when it is over
when the dying is nearly done
when the blood as dark as winter
chokes my baleen plates,
That the darkness is my own."

"He's singing," says Tat again. She puts her hands on the whale's scalloped flipper. Her necklace of jingle shells rattles on her chest. And from her mouth, like a whisper, come the whale sounds, the whistles and groans. But they're faint now, and faltering.

" Hear me sing of this
how I bore my child along
my dying and bleeding child.
On my back I carried her and let her
breathe the air.
And when she died I carried her
my back to serve as land
until her flesh in rotting strips brought
sharks
with tearing teeth.
And only then I let her go. I let her fall away
and rolled with aching flukes to watch

her spiral to a grave
Oh, God. Don't let me drown."

Murray has read only a little part of what goes on for pages, but he closes the book, holds it for a moment, then passes it back to Squid. He looks up and blows a long breath toward the sky and the circling birds. He closes his eyes, breathes in and out again, then stands beside the whale, stroking it softly. Hannah stands with him until the humpback dies with a rasping of air, and Tat's little song fades off into nothing.

The enormous eyes don't close; Hannah doesn't know if they can. But they lose their depth, their wildness and their light. It goes from them like the snuffing of a candle.

In silence, they start up toward the house. Murray will call someone. A boat—or a chopper—will come, and the men will bring chain saws.

⁓

On Squid's first day, Hannah held on to her arm. Now she does it again, slowing her down on the boardwalk. This time, Squid does not pull away.

"Mom," she says, "I'm leaving the island today. When the boat comes, I'm taking Tat. I'm going home, Mom."

The choice of her words has a poignancy for Hannah. Never again will Squid talk of Lizzie as home.

"I might come back," says Squid. "I don't know. But I have to go home. There are too many ghosts on the island."

Hannah squeezes her arm. "Now you know how I feel."

Every year it's the same. She tells herself it's the rain

and the darkness, the weary forever of winter. But she flies from the island when the snow starts to fall. She's afraid to see the ground covered in white, afraid she'll find tracks in the morning when the footsteps go by in the night. When the voices cry out from the past.

Not always is it Alastair. Again and again she wakes in her bed, hearing doors banging open and Squid shrieking, "Mom!" And she bolts up in her bed, sure that Squid will come flying into the room. She'll be six months pregnant, her nightgown stained with blood.

"Mom?" asks Squid. "On the night that Alastair died, did you hear him playing his flute?"

"Yes." Hannah *still* hears the flute when the nights are crisp and wintery. But that night the music was different; it was weeping with sadness.

"He had it with him," says Squid. "But it's back. It's up in his room."

"Murray found it." Hannah bumps against Squid where the boardwalk turns through the trees. She looks back, and sees how the birds are falling from the sky, settling down by the corpse of the whale. "He went everywhere," she says. "Round and round the island, out to every reef and rock. He rowed the little boat and looked down through the glass, and—Squid—the look on his face when he passed over forests of kelp . . ." Hannah shivers. "The flute was lying on the beach. Half buried in the sand."

It was only a week after Alastair died. Murray brought it up to the house as she worked in the kitchen. He couldn't resist playing it. He tootled some notes as he passed by the window. For that moment—that instant— she forgot that Alastair was dead. And the joy she felt, as she looked out to see him—before she saw Murray in- stead . . . Well, she hadn't felt that happy even one more time in all the years gone by.

"He was playing on the beach that night," she says to Squid. "I think he went to the place that he liked best as a boy. It's funny how it all goes in circles. That was probably the place where I landed my kayak; maybe the place where Erik brought his."

Suddenly, Squid is sniffling.

"What's wrong?" asks Hannah.

"It was silly," says Squid. "I saw his flute and started to think that maybe he wasn't really dead. That he'd just gone away like he always did. That he was living on the is- land somewhere. On the island or the atoll."

"I used to think that too," says Hannah. She thought it all the time. Her first winter off the island, she felt *wrong* to go. She was abandoning her son, she thought.

They're deeper in the forest now, higher on the island. The trees whisper in a wind. And Hannah hears its voice. She starts, and her hand tightens under her daughter's arm. But Squid keeps walking. The wind talks only to Hannah.

They pass the ribbons marking Murray's house of fancy, the one he'll never build. There's another turn in the board- walk, and the ending comes into view, like a tunnel mouth to a world of green and sunlight. In minutes they'll be home.

"Squid?" says Hannah.

"Hmm?"

"Do you think I'm awful for leaving your father alone in the winter?"

"No," says Squid.

"And Alastair? Do you think he'd be angry?"

Squid walks along, holding the notebook against her chest. "Not *angry*," she says at last. "He'd be disappointed, maybe. He wanted us all to be happy. He wanted everyone to be happy and safe."

Hannah nods to herself. She's known that all along.

"I hurt him so much," says Squid. "I didn't know that before, how much I hurt him. I just destroyed him in the end."

"Don't say that," says Hannah.

"But I did, Mom. He wrote it all in his books, everything I said, and—"

"I mean it," says Hannah. "This is water under the bridge. You did everything you could for him."

"But it wasn't enough," says Squid, almost whining. "He wrote about that. He wrote about *you*. He wrote about—"

Hannah pulls the book from Squid's hands. "I don't want to *know* what he wrote about."

"Why not?"

"Because it won't bring him back, will it? It can't help *him*, but it might hurt *me*, so it wouldn't do anyone any good." Hannah holds the book firmly, not even tempted to open it. "I'm frightened of it, Squid."

"The others aren't so bad," says Squid.

"There's others?"

Squid nods. "Eight books in all. He hid them in his floor."

"Show me," says Hannah.

"I thought you didn't—"

"I *don't*." Hannah grabs her daughter's arm and pulls her along. "I want to get rid of them, Squid. I want them out of there before Murray thinks of looking for them."

chapter
seventeen

SQUID GLANCES UP AS SHE COMES OUT
from the forest. The tower is sparkling white in the sun,
the sky above it blue and clear. Murray's lawns glisten
with moisture, and Lizzie Island seems somehow fresh.
Somehow new. Squid smiles, feeling happy—though she
doesn't know why—for the first time since she arrived on
the *Darby*. She breathes the smell of sea and grass and
trees, then starts forward again, looking down at the
boardwalk and the planks that flash past her feet.

Then she steps down onto gravel, the boardwalk ending where the lawn begins, and she links her arm through
her mom's. Now that she knows she's leaving, she wishes
she could stay. For a tiny fraction of a moment, she wishes
that with all her heart.

Murray comes up from behind as they walk the last
few yards to the small house. Squid steps off to the left,
and her mom to the right, and Murray trots between
them, breathing hard, with little Tatiana riding on his
shoulders. Her dark hair is blowing back from her face,

and she grins down at her mother. But she doesn't let go of Murray.

"The weathers," he says as he passes, his boots crunching in the gravel. "I nearly forgot the weathers again." On he goes, along the paths, toward the sunshine and the tower. "Tatty's going to help," he calls back, between breaths that come in puffs.

Squid remembers being carried like that. She remembers the smell of her father's clothes, always clean no matter what oily business he'd been up to. She remembers the feeling of being carried so high, and so safely. It makes her sad to see how much more slowly her father runs now.

At the small house she starts up the steps. Suddenly her mother is behind her instead of beside her, and she looks down from the porch. "Are you sure you want to see this?"

"Yes," says Hannah. She's staring at the sign above the door, Alastair's handwritten Gomorrah. "I think I can go in there now," she says.

They don't linger in the living room. They go straight to the upper floor, then turn to the right into Alastair's room. Squid, in her hurry, left the mat pulled aside, the floorboards open. The dark spines of Alastair's books stand up in a line in the hole.

"There's so many," says Hannah. She gets to her knees and lifts out the first one. "Oh, dear," she says. "Do you think this is right, to get rid of them?"

"I don't know," says Squid.

"Are they that bad? Did they make you cry?"

"Yes," says Squid. "Sometimes I laughed, but mostly I cried."

"Then help me." Hannah pulls out the books three at a time. "There's too many to burn. We'll have to dig a hole and bury them."

"You could leave them where they are."

"No," says Hannah. "You found them; so will Murray. Or the next keeper, or the one after that. I just want to lay all this to rest."

"Okay," says Squid. She arranges the books in a pile, and when the last one's out her mother reaches deep in the floor, her fingers scratching at the wood. A spiderweb breaks loose with a tiny shredding sound.

"There's nothing else," says Hannah. "Now hurry. Your father won't take very long with the weathers."

They close the floorboards, then slide the mat into place. They carry the books down the stairs and out from Gomorrah. Hunched over, half running, they scurry round the small house and into the forest. At a patch of clear ground, in a ring of hemlock trees, they drop to the ground and dig with their hands, through the moss and the loam. They scrape out a hollow just deep enough for Alastair's books, and lay them down on the black soil.

For Squid it's like a funeral, like the service they never had for her brother. The sound of the surf is in the distance; there are birds singing in the trees. Visions of Alastair flicker through her mind—his face, his voice, his laughter. She is carried through years before she finds herself back in the forest.

Across the scar they've made in the moss, her mother is hunched over the broken ground. Her hands, stained black from the earth, are spread flat across the notebooks. "He wrote everything in these?" she asks. "About me and Murray and you?"

"Yes."

"And Erik? Did he write about Erik?"

"Yes, Mom. A bit."

"Just the way you told me? How Erik came in his kayak, and how you made him think mermaids were real? All of that's here?"

"Some of it."

"But all of it's true, isn't it?"

"Mom, don't," says Squid. She doesn't want to start on this, examining each little part of what happened. She's afraid that one question will lead to another, and there are things she will never talk about to anybody. "Erik was real; he was here. I don't want to think about the stuff that happened after."

"All right," says Hannah. There are streaks of mud, like black tears, on her face, but she looks happier. "I've imagined so many horrors. Oh, Squid, I'm so sorry for everything."

They hug across the hole, their cheeks touching, their foreheads on each other's shoulders. They lean together, breathing together, until neither can move without both of them collapsing into the hole. Slowly, they topple sideways onto the moss, giggling with their arms entangled.

Squid pushes herself up. But Hannah just lies there, sprawled on the ground, still laughing as she stares at the sky. She sweeps her arms around and makes a pillow from her hands. "I think something's finished," she says. "Something's over. I feel good again, Squid."

"Me too. I'm glad I came back." Squid scoops dirt from the moss and casts it over the books. She starts with big, double handfuls and makes a mound over Alastair's things, then pats it down and starts again, until she's scraping with her fingers for the last bits of black on the green. The moss goes on top, and her mother helps her then, folding the shredded pieces back in their places again.

When they finish, the ground looks bruised. When they stand, their clothes are covered with bits of moss, their skin with stains of dirt. "We can't let Murray see us like this," says Hannah. So instead of going back they go forward, through the forest and down to the sea. They wash their hands and faces, catching the waves that tumble toward them, surging up the rocks. They each pick the moss from the other's clothes, then walk side by side to the big house.

Murray has finished the weathers. He's at his endless task of clearing debris from the lawn and the paths. He's using his garden rake with its long steel fingers to sweep along the wailing wall. And he's put Tatiana to work. She snatches up the leaves and twigs as he drags them out, and she squashes them into a tidy little pile.

Squid watches them as she walks closer. There's a sparrow on the lawn a yard away, a junco close behind it. A Steller's jay, with its cheeky little topknot, hops along the stones. Murray twists his rake along the little wall, and Tatiana pounces on the leaves.

"That's seven now," says Murray.

"Then ten?" asks Tat, looking up.

"No, no. We've got eight and nine to go before we get to ten."

Tatiana sighs. "Och, it's a big number."

Squid laughs. Murray looks up and sees her there with Hannah.

"What's going on?" says Squid.

Murray turns his rake upside down and puts the end of the handle on the path. "Every ten sweeps, we take what we have and throw it over the cliff," he says. "That's Tat's favorite part, isn't it, Tatty?"

She nods, still gathering leaves. Then she leans closer to the stones, grimaces, and shrieks, "Look! Oh, Grandpa, look!"

Murray puts down his rake and kneels beside her. Tatiana's finger is shaking so much that it's hard to tell where she's pointing. But Murray squints and bobs his head. "Och," he says. "That's just a spider. Has she never seen a spider, Squid?"

"I don't point them out," says Squid.

"Well, you should." Murray opens his arms. "Gather round."

They close around him, just as they did years before, Squid at his side and Hannah at his back, little Tatiana in Alastair's place close in front of him.

"He's a clever little fellow," Murray says. "A fisherman, born and bred. See his net, anchored there and there and there? He fishes the sky, not the sea."

Squid leans closer, her hand on her father's shoulder.

"He started out as just a wee thing," says Murray. "Scores of baby spiders could sit on your fingertip, Tat."

Tatiana holds her finger inches from her eyes.

"Then, one day, he floats away. He goes soaring off on a bit of thread, wherever the winds might blow him. And as soon as he's down he goes to work, casting his net from a twig or a stone or a blade of grass. No one's ever taught him how to do it, but he knows. This miracle is inside him, in his wee speck of a brain. He sets out his anchors, then weaves his net, and there he sits, as patient as Job. No skulking through the forest for this fellow, he lets his dinner come to him. But he's no layabout, either. Just watch."

Murray picks among the stones and finds a bit of old twig half an inch long. He holds it up for all of them to see, then tosses it forward, and it snags on the spider's web. The instant it hits, the spider is there.

"Fast as lightning, isn't he?" says Murray. "Now he's seen through my trick already. He knows it's just a bit of twig. But he's not about to leave it hanging there. Tell me why not."

"The flies might see it!" shouts Squid. Then she blushes when her mother laughs.

"Right you are," says Murray. "His net is very special. It's—"

"Invisible," says Tatiana. She looks up with her eyes huge. "It's invisible, Grandpa."

"Good girl, Tat." He ruffles her hair. "You're as sharp as that spider, I think. Yes, his threads are so fine that even a fly can't see them. But if a bit of wind—or some clod like me—comes along and fills the net with old sticks, then he's not going to catch many flies, is he? So he cuts it loose."

They all watch as the spider works, its eight legs busy at once, snipping the threads and prying at the twig. It levers the twig away from the web, then drops it clear to the ground. And it sets to work repairing the damage, fixing its perfect web.

"That's his life's work," says Murray. "Tending his net. We won't put him to the bother, of course, but if we broke his anchors and let his net collapse, he'd bustle about with his strings and his glue until he was all set up again. No rest for him, no time for play. He's a very serious fellow. For him it's always work first . . ."

Murray falls silent, staring at the web. Squid imagines him thinking of all the sunny mornings spent at lighthouse chores, the rainy afternoons left for sodden play. She presses harder on his back, kneading at his muscles. "But he does the best he can," she says softly.

"Aye, he does." Murray scratches his ear. "Och, he's a simple sort of soul, I suppose." Then he sighs and shifts himself straighter. His voice becomes louder, more cheerful. "Well, any questions? Then—"

"Yes," says Squid. "Can Tatiana stay with you?"

"What?" says Murray. Hannah, too, looks up.

Squid forges ahead; it's too late to go back. "Dad, I have to go home," she says.

"Now?" His shoulders slump. His hands settle, and tighten, on Tatiana's shoulders. "You're leaving already?"

"Yes, Dad. I *have* to, but Tatiana could stay for the month, just for the month that I promised." She's glad that she can't see her father's face. "Then we're going to Australia, Dad. I'm sorry I didn't tell you sooner, but— well, I'm getting married and we're going to Australia. But Tat could stay here for the month." Then she asks Tatiana, just as quickly, "Would you like that, baby? Would you like to stay a bit longer with your grandma and your grandpa?"

"Ooh, yes," says Tat, grinning already.

"If your grandma says it's all right. Whatever your grandma thinks."

Squid looks at Hannah. There's still a tiny bit of moss stuck in her hair. Hannah looks back, wondering at first, and then smiling. "That sounds lovely," she says. "I could even bring Tatiana down to Vancouver. When I leave for the mainland."

"That would be great," says Squid. "Dad, what do you think?"

Murray's still watching the spider. He nods quite slowly. "It's not what I hoped for," he says. "But, och, it will be a grand month."

chapter eighteen

*T*HE UNDERTAKER ARRIVES JUST BEFORE SUN-set. He comes from the east, low on the water, croaking his raven's cry. Squid looks up at the sound, and watches as he settles on the red cap of the tower, a little black figure high above the lawns and the buildings.

He's been coming to Lizzie Island for as long as she can remember; before she was born he was coming each fall. He's old and ragged; he has only one leg. But there he'll stand, day and night, waiting for the fog and the song-birds.

Alastair hated the Undertaker. "That black thing," he called it. "I'm going to kill that black thing," he vowed one year, and he spent hours standing below the tower, flinging stones in every direction. He could hardly *see* the raven, let alone hit it.

Murray took him away, probably frightened of a win-dow getting broken, or the tower paint being chipped. He brought Alastair back and sat him in the kitchen. "It's all part of nature," he said. "Another link in the chain. That raven has a purpose here, just like you and me and every creature on the island."

"But he doesn't have to *like* it," said Alastair.

It was tragic, what happened. In the fog, or on dark and rainy nights, the songbirds passing in hordes to the south were drawn to the twirling beacon. They smashed against the glass and the concrete, and their bodies piled up on the platform or tumbled to the rocks. They covered the ground some mornings, their necks snapped, their wings broken, their bright little breasts heaving. And then the Undertaker came down from the tower and feasted on the corpses.

Even now Squid feels a sickness in her stomach to see him arrive, black as a shadow, swooping up to his perch. She's sitting on the winch pad, brushing Tatiana's hair, but she stops to watch the raven.

"Ah, here he is," says Murray, beside her. "You see that, Hannah?"

"Yes, Murray. I'm not blind."

Squid is sitting on her suitcase with Tatiana balanced on its edge in front of her. Murray on her left, Hannah on her right, they're sitting in a row, leaning on the rocks. Below them, the *Cloo Stung* is tethered to the mooring buoy, looking square and squat from above. It's far smaller than the *Darby*, but faster. For nearly an hour its inflatable boat has been going back and forth to the little lagoon, where the sound of a chain saw buzzes through the forest. The sound carries well in the twilight calm.

"Do you remember what Alastair got you to do?" asks Hannah.

"Yes," says Squid. "It didn't work any better than his other ideas."

He gathered cedar boughs, bundles and bundles of them. He whined and snorted until she helped him, and they packed the boughs to the top of the tower. They padded the railings and the hard edge of the platform, lashing down the branches with bits of string and rope. But the songbirds died in numbers even greater than before.

"Maybe we should ask Dad to turn off the beacon," said Alastair.

"Good idea, Dumbo," she said. "You can stand here all night with your stupid little oil light."

She grimaces now, remembering that. There were so many times when she hurt him.

The cabin door opens on the *Cloo Stung*. A uniformed man comes out with a saucepan that he empties over the side. He clanks a spoon around inside it, and the Undertaker echoes the sound. The man looks up, clanks again, but the raven doesn't answer anymore. The man shrugs, then turns toward the landing. "We'll be leaving very soon," he shouts.

Squid waves, the brush held high in her hand.

She watches the man step back into the cabin, then takes the brush to Tatiana's hair. Each stroke sizzles through the dark strands, tugging the child's head to the left or the right.

"He's early this year," says Murray, still looking up at the tower.

"You think so?" asks Hannah.

Murray nods. "Last year you were already gone when he came."

"No I wasn't. I remember counting birds, hoping to find at least one I could rescue."

"Really? Och, you could be right," says Murray. "But you leave a little sooner every year."

Squid puts down the brush and smooths Tat's hair with her fingers. She covers the child's ears and tells Murray, softly, "Don't let her watch the Undertaker. And please keep her away from the beach until they've finished with the whale."

"Fair enough," says Murray.

"Remember to cut her toast into fingers, and don't let her wander too close to the cliffs. Don't drive her too fast in the wagon, okay, Dad? And keep her away from the bridge when it's stormy. And away from the sea when it's rough."

Murray produces an imaginary pencil in his fingers. His tongue comes out, as though licking the tip, and he writes out a list in the air, over his hand. He speaks each line as he writes:

"Don't let

Tatiana

have any

fun."

"Oh, Dad," says Squid, laughing. She gives Tatiana a playful shake. "You know what I mean."

"Yes, and I'll watch her," he says. "Be assured of that. But I didn't go all that far wrong with you, did I? Och, I wasn't perfect, God knows, but you've grown into a fine, good woman nonetheless."

Squid blushes, suddenly teary. That's the highest compliment that Murray has ever paid her. She tickles Tatiana's ribs, and the child giggles. One more brush at her hair, one more hug, then Squid passes her daughter into Murray's care.

His huge hands hold her firmly. "The wee Tatty will be happy here, while you're gone," he says. "And she'll be just as happy to leave again."

"I doubt it," says Squid.

Hannah clucks her tongue. "Of course she will."

"But when I was her age," says Squid, "I wanted to stay here forever. I thought it was paradise."

"And it is," says Murray. "It's Eden, right enough: full of beauty and knowledge, a fine place to start from." He wraps Tatiana in his thick, strong arms and gazes at the sea that stretches on nearly forever. "But I suppose there's always a time for leaving."

Squid leans against him, feeling his breath and his heartbeat. Her own time for leaving is just a few minutes off, and now she wishes it was farther. "What will you do tomorrow?" she asks.

"Och, where to start?" says Murray. "We've got the whole small house to clean up. We've got to find that Barney doll; lord knows where it's gone. There are paths to clear, and the steps will want painting—"

"Play sandbox!" shouts Tatiana.

"Oh, yes," says Murray. "That's the first thing."

"Play first, work after?" teases Squid.

"Why not?" says Murray. "Just this once, though, mind."

The chain saw stops, and a motor starts up. Then the workboat passes, full of men and thick bundles. It sidles up to the *Cloo Stung*, and when the outboard shuts down, there are only the sounds of the sea and the island. Then the big engines of the *Cloo Stung* roar and gurgle. The men clamber from the boat, and it's hoisted aboard, the cargo still inside, the outboard dripping water from its leg.

The sky is dark and tinged with orange, the water nearly purple. The *Cloo Stung*'s lights come on, a glaring red on the side toward the island.

"I guess I've got to go," says Squid. She grabs Tatiana. "Now, listen," she says. "You do what you're told, you hear? And you stay away—"

"Och, you've told her all that," says Murray.

"Okay," says Squid. "I'll see you soon, Tatiana." She kisses her daughter, then stands up.

Hannah rises on her right, Murray on her left. He holds out his arm as though he means only to shake hands. "I'm very proud of you, Squid," he says.

She throws herself at him and he hugs her back, his arms like sticks at first, until they bend and tighten round her shoulders. Her tears run onto his collar. "I'm glad I came back," she says. "I'm sorry I disappeared."

"It's all right," he says. "Squid, it's all right."

The *Cloo Stung*'s horn blasts with a tuneless screech. In a swirl of smoke, a rush of dark water, the boat backs away from the mooring.

Squid turns from Murray to Hannah, everything she can see just a blur and a shimmer. Her mother hugs her fiercely, more tightly than she's ever been held before. "Don't say anything, Squid," she says. "We'll see you soon, Tatiana and I."

Squid steps back, wiping at her nose with the back of her hand. Her throat feels sore, her eyes on fire. She picks up her suitcase and starts down to the sea.

The *Cloo Stung* is small enough to come right to the shore. The skipper maneuvers from the deck, swinging his boat in the channel, going astern toward the steps. He nudges a lever; water boils at the stern, rushing over the concrete.

Squid looks down, looks back at Tatiana huddled up to Murray's leg. She drops her suitcase. A wave of her arms will send the boat away, will leave her on the island with her daughter and her parents. She can still stay until the end of the month. She spreads her arms wide and Tat runs toward her, thumping into her knees.

"Oh, my baby," she says.

She's ready to shout, to send the *Cloo Stung* on its way. But she'll have to sleep in the small house. She'll have to fill it again with a child's laugh, with a child's games and stories at bedtime. She'll have to bunk with Alastair's ghost, seeing his face wherever she looks, hearing his voice whenever she turns.

Her arms, already half-raised, fall instead for one last touch of her daughter's hair, for one more hug. Then she takes up the suitcase again and marches down the steps.

Three men help her over the transom and onto the deck. They hold her up by her elbows as though she's a frail old lady. The skipper smiles, then pushes the throttle. And the boat slides forward, leaving the island behind.

Her eyes are still blurry with tears. Her father is a big, pink blob on the landing, her mother a smear of brown and red, her daughter a tiny, tiny thing. In a moment they're gone, hidden by the turn in the cliff.

The *Cloo Stung* travels so fast that it banks when it turns. It rises on the waves with a steamy spray at the stern. In moments it has passed the last reef, swinging to the south, bashing into the seas with foam churning between the twin hulls.

One by one, the crew slip into the cabin. But Squid stays in the stern, watching the island shrink.

It's darker than the sea and darker than the sky, a hunched shape like an animal sleeping. There's a square of yellow light from a window of the big house, but soon that is gone, hidden by the trees. Then only the beacon is there, flashing across the water, flashing again. Squid can feel her heart beating with it, keeping time to the Lizzie light.

The *Cloo Stung* carries her away, pitching across the black slopes of the swells. The beacon sinks below the water, and the wind lashes at the lightkeeper's daughter.

Acknowledgments

Lizzie Island isn't real, but there is a place just like it. It's called Lucy Island, and it lies just west of Prince Rupert. I have walked along its beaches and through its forest, following the boardwalk from the beach to the tower, past the midden and the meadow. I have anchored in its sandy lagoon, and watched the auklets arrive at sunset.

There was once a lighthouse there, and a lightkeeper with a family of young children. I never knew their names, though I met them once or twice. They left the island many years ago, when the lighthouse was automated and the little white-and-red houses were burned to the ground. This story is not about them.

I sometimes regret turning Lucy Island into a fictional setting for tragedy. It was, and is, one of my favorite places.

The factual information for this story came from two friends, both longtime keepers of the lights. Larry Golden, who has tended to the lonely rock of Triple Island for more than twenty-five years, provided many details about the workings of a lightstation and the realities of a lightkeeper's life. Chris Mills, who has worked on lights on both the east coast and the west, and who now is deeply involved in preserving east-coast stations, read the manuscript in an early form, made corrections, and suggested improvements. He gave me a tour of the light at Dryad Point, on the Inside Passage of British Columbia's coast. To these two friends, I owe many thanks.

About the Author

IAIN LAWRENCE studied journalism in Vancouver, British Columbia, and worked for small newspapers in the northern part of the province. He settled on the coast, living first in the port city of Prince Rupert and then at a remote radio-transmitter site that could be reached only by boat or helicopter. He now lives on the Gulf Islands. An avid sailor, Iain Lawrence wrote two nonfiction books about his travels on the coast before turning to children's novels. *The Lightkeeper's Daughter* is set on the north coast, where the remains of a lighthouse stand on an island very much like the fictional Lizzie.

Iain Lawrence is the author of five other novels for young readers, including the acclaimed High Seas Trilogy: *The Wreckers* (an Edgar Allan Poe Award nominee), *The Smugglers*, and *The Buccaneers*. Lawrence's *Ghost Boy*, set in postwar America, was named a *Publishers Weekly* Best Book of the Year, a *School Library Journal* Best Book of the Year, an ALA Best Book for Young Adults, and an ALA Notable Book. *Lord of the Nutcracker Men*, inspired in part by family stories of Iain Lawrence's grandfather, was named a *Publishers Weekly* Best Book of the Year and a *School Library Journal* Best Book of the Year.